THE TIME
BEFORE NOW

By the Author

All Things Rise

The Ground Beneath

The Time Before Now

Visit us at www.boldstrokesbooks.com

THE TIME
BEFORE NOW

by
Missouri Vaun

2015

THE TIME BEFORE NOW
© 2015 By Missouri Vaun. All Rights Reserved.

ISBN 13: 978-1-62639-446-9

This Trade Paperback Original Is Published By
Bold Strokes Books, Inc.
P.O. Box 249
Valley Falls, NY 12185

First Edition: October 2015

CREDITS
EDITOR: CINDY CRESAP
PRODUCTION DESIGN: STACIA SEAMAN
CHARACTER ILLUSTRATION BY: PAIGE BRADDOCK
COVER DESIGN BY SHERI (GRAPHICARTIST2020@HOTMAIL.COM)

Acknowledgments

This book was pretty far along by the time I attended a writer's retreat in Spain led by Victoria Villasenor. I say it was pretty far along, and what I should say is that it was pretty far along the wrong track. I owe Victoria a big thank you for the reality check she gave me in terms of plot structure. And thanks to Michelle Green, my writing comrade during this retreat, who also agreed to beta read for me once I'd gotten the story back on the right path. Your insights about injury and recovery times were very helpful.

D. Jackson Leigh offered great feedback about the sections involving horses. In general, Deb has given me great writing advice and has challenged me to be better. Thank you for your friendship and support.

Thanks also to Vanessa, Alena, Art, and Celina. You guys have offered feedback and encouragement all along the writing process and I really appreciate it.

I'd also like to thank Radclyffe, Sandy, and Ruth from Bold Strokes Books. A special thanks to my editor, Cindy; your Star Wars analogies make total sense to me. You make the editing process fun.

Lastly, I'd like to extend loving thanks to my wife, Evelyn. Your notes and your patience and support during my late-night writing binges have made this whole dream come true. I love you.

For my Cherokee ancestors.

CHAPTER ONE

Vivian Wildfire Yates raised the brim of her Stetson to scan the dusty landscape. She could barely make out the cloud city of Houston over the distance between where she stood and where it hovered near the horizon. Its enormous floating silhouette was hardly visible against the cobalt sky, like some faraway mountaintop untethered from the earth. In a different lifetime, in a different era, maybe she'd have been up there instead of down here, but not in this life.

Vivian pulled up the bandana around her neck to shield her face from the new dust devil that formed outside the animal enclosure where she was standing. Green pastures had once been the norm across the Southeast Texas Territory, or so her grandfather had told her. But that was over a hundred years ago, before peak oil and before the depletion of the huge natural aquifer that once resided under the middle of the entire Midwestern region. Now, in the spring of 2185, fossil fuels were only remembered in history books.

The land spreading out to the west was like an open palm baking in the merciless noontime heat. It was practically uninhabitable. As a result, those who dwelt nearby clung to the eastern edge of the Texas Territory, where the possibility of some limited cattle grazing and fresh water still existed. Oklahoma to the north, where Vivian had migrated from just over a month ago, was worse off than East Texas. Even still, this country, dry and nearly barren, was Eden compared to parts farther west where the ever-expanding desert made it impossible for anything or anyone to live.

The midday sun had settled high in the arid sky. The unfiltered sunlight peeked under the lip of Vivian's hat, momentarily blinding her. She lowered her hat and settled back into the task at hand. She primed the pump handle again, sloshing water into the deep wood-hewn trough where several thin and thirsty cattle gathered expectantly.

Vivian left Oklahoma Territory after her grandfather had passed. He was the last remnant of family holding her in place and was one of only a few tribal elders of the Cherokee Nation who kept their oral traditions alive. Frequently since his passing, his words would come back to her. *In the beginning, there was only darkness and water.* Now there seemed to be only heat and dust.

Vivian had left with nothing but what little possessions she could carry in a knapsack over her shoulder. She had decided to head east in search of her grandfather's ancestral home in the Blue Mountains. Her ancestral home. She had walked southeasterly for days, picking up odd jobs along the way for food and board. Vivian had never known a time when hard currency existed. Barter was the only economy she and generations before her had known. The only real commodities in this modern age were land, houses, grain, cattle, and survival skills.

After several days, Vivian stumbled onto the Hudson Ranch. They were looking for hands to tend cattle and to do other light farm tasks. Vivian, being more masculine than feminine in both stature and habits, asked for work and was accepted. That was little more than two weeks ago, and now she thought each day should be her last. She needed to continue her journey. But the truth was she still felt tired from the ground she'd just covered, and a few more days of steady meals and shelter might put her in the right spirits to continue her move toward the sunrise.

If she were honest with herself, Vivian reckoned that there might be a reason besides fatigue that slowed her departure. She raised her head just enough to observe discreetly as that *reason* moved across the large patch of dry earth in front of the Hudsons' main house. Vivian's direct gaze hid beneath the shadow of her hat as Elizabeth Hudson pulled her chestnut-colored mare to a stop several feet from the porch. She dismounted in one swift movement and loosely draped the reins around a post before trotting up and into the house.

Vivian had allowed her mind to drift, until a shadow fell across where she stood. Walt Hudson was looking at her with a frown, as if he'd just eaten something sour.

"Stop daydreaming, Yates. Finish here and get those cows in the south pasture up here and out of the heat," Walt demanded. "And then go help Anders haul hay to the barn."

His posture conveyed arrogance and so did his left boot on the edge of the water trough. He paused long enough to spit into the dirt and look back at Vivian before he turned toward the house.

"Yes, sir," said Vivian.

Walt was one of the main reasons she shouldn't linger on the Hudson Ranch. Despite the fact that she was at least two inches taller than Walt at nearly six feet, he still managed to look down on her. His every directive was delivered with the intention to make her feel small. How he could be the brother of someone as pretty as Elizabeth defied genetics. She shook her head as she gave the pump one last downward stroke.

Vivian pushed thoughts of Elizabeth from her mind. *Stay focused. Get fit, rested, and keep moving.* Vivian needed to make this her mantra. Pining over the fetching Elizabeth Hudson would never amount to anything. Her daydreams and late-night fantasies were only serving to delay her departure plans and nothing more.

Vivian's back was toward the house, but she turned as she heard footsteps approach. She figured it was Walt back to give her more orders.

"Would you mind seeing to my horse?" Elizabeth asked, holding the reins out to Vivian.

"Sure." Vivian feared that the look on her face communicated her earlier internal monologue. It was almost as if her musings had called Elizabeth forth.

"You can take the reins. I won't bite." One side of Elizabeth's mouth curled up into a smile.

Vivian took a moment to savor Elizabeth's green eyes, fair

skin, and shoulder-length brown hair shimmering in the sun's rays. Vivian couldn't help but notice how the sun practically danced in her sparkling green irises. As was her habit, Elizabeth wore a fitted blouse and snug riding pants with tall black boots.

Get it together. Stop staring. Vivian reached for the narrow leather straps. "I'll take care of her."

Vivian took the reins and led the horse into the weathered barn's dark interior, pausing to run her fingers through her thick damp hair and adjust her hat. Vivian patted the horse's dusty neck once and got her into the stall. She removed the saddle and blanket, and set a bucket of water and grain near the back of the stall. It wasn't until she'd placed the saddle on its rack that she turned and realized Elizabeth was standing beside her. Vivian froze. A combination of excitement and panic rose in the pit of her stomach, and she was sure the look on her face was something akin to a spooked deer.

Elizabeth reached over to place her hand on Vivian's forearm, exposed below her turned-up shirtsleeve. The contrast of Elizabeth's delicate, slender fingers against Vivian's sinewy, tanned forearm was striking, as if further emphasizing their differences.

"I wondered if you could help me with something." Elizabeth was looking down, her eyes focused on the spot where her fingertips brushed across Vivian's skin. "Something in the house."

Heat registered under Elizabeth's fingers on her arm. Vivian was struggling to decipher what she was feeling about both the touch and the request. Every fiber in Vivian's body was sending her a warning signal. But Vivian knew that whatever Elizabeth requested, she would be powerless to refuse. Vivian still remained hopeful that it was something as innocent and mundane as catching a feral cat who'd found itself trapped in the pantry. Somehow, she figured that wouldn't be the case.

"Sure. What do you need help with?"

"Come with me and I'll show you."

Vivian had only been inside the main Hudson house twice, and both times only through the back door and into the kitchen. This time she followed Elizabeth up the front steps and into the sitting room. She was glad to take notice that Walt was nowhere in sight as she closed the front door behind them. Upon entering, Vivian stopped, looking down at the cleanly polished plank floors and at her muck-covered boots. Elizabeth turned and responded to Vivian's questioning look. "Just take them off and leave them by the door."

Vivian sat on a bench along the foyer's wall and slipped off her worn boots. Unfortunately, her boots had protected her from revealing the sad condition of her socks. Large holes ventilated each of her toes.

"I could mend those for you," said Elizabeth.

"That's kind of you. I can mend them. I should have done it already." Vivian cleared her throat, set her hat on the bench, and stood to follow Elizabeth down the long entry hallway and up the stairs to the second floor, quietly padding along.

"In here." Elizabeth motioned for Vivian to follow her into one of the upstairs rooms, and once inside, she opened the door to a rather tall closet. She pointed to a wooden box sitting on the top shelf. "That's my problem. I wondered if you could reach it for me?"

Vivian realized she wasn't offering any service that a well-placed chair couldn't accommodate, but she was flattered and at the same time excited to have something that Elizabeth needed. In this case, five or six extra inches and maybe some added upper-body strength.

Elizabeth stepped aside so that Vivian could move past her into the small space. As she reached up to retrieve the box off the top shelf, Vivian became hyperaware of Elizabeth's nearness. Vivian let the box fall back onto the shelf and lowered her arms slowly, as if trying not to spook the beautiful young woman staring up at her. Elizabeth reciprocated by sliding her hands down Vivian's rib cage. Both of them exhaled sharply at the physical contact.

"What are you doing?" Vivian kept her hands up and out at her sides, as if waiting to catch something that was about to fall.

Elizabeth grabbed Vivian's shirt, just above where it was tucked into her belt. "What does it seem like I'm doing?"

"Whatever it is, it's not a good idea." Vivian said the words even though they were at odds with her heart, and her libido.

She felt Elizabeth release her shirt and step away from her. The loss of contact stirred something in Vivian. Why was she worried? They were alone, and obviously there was a mutual attraction. She took Elizabeth firmly by the shoulders and kissed her hard. She felt the softness of Elizabeth's breasts press into her chest as she leaned into her against the back wall of the closet. Vivian came to her senses after a few seconds, pulling her lips away, breathing hard, only to have Elizabeth close the space between them again.

An alarm sounded somewhere in the back of Vivian's hormone-addled brain, and she pulled away again. She envisioned Walt bursting in on them, not the least bit happy to find his baby sister making out with the hired help.

"I'm sorry. I shouldn't have done that," said Vivian. She ran her fingers through her hair to calm herself.

"Don't be sorry." Elizabeth was still leaning against the rough boards at the back of the closet. It was hard to read the expression on her face, but Vivian was fairly certain it wasn't regret.

Vivian stood awkwardly, not sure what to do next. Elizabeth stepped around her and pulled the door to the bedroom closed. The click of the latch snapped loudly in Vivian's head, although she knew in reality there'd hardly been any sound.

"Do you need help with something else?"

"Yes, I do." Elizabeth's hand moved from the doorknob to the buttons of her fitted white blouse. She released the fasteners that Vivian noticed earlier had been straining over her full breasts. Vivian couldn't help allowing her eyes to linger on the buxom cleavage as the buttons of Elizabeth's shirt gave way.

This wasn't the first time a woman had asked for assistance with this particular thing. Vivian was lucky enough to have something that women seemed to be drawn to. It started when she was in her late teens and had not lessened in frequency. But for some reason, this felt different. Elizabeth slipped out of her shirt and her bra before she worked on the buttons of Vivian's trousers. Vivian couldn't help feeling a little like the fly who falls in pooled nectar at the bottom of a beautiful carnivorous plant right before she's about to be eaten.

CHAPTER TWO

Ida leaned against the porch railing and sighed. She would miss the view of the water, but not enough to stay. She heard footsteps behind her and turned, smiling at Kate, who approached carrying two cups of steaming tea.

"I love this view in the early morning." Kate cradled the warm cup in both hands as she sipped the hot liquid. Ida noticed her hands wore several small cuts and scrapes from her woodworking.

"Is John up?" Ida asked.

"He left really early. Something about helping his friend Jason with a barn repair. I think I was too sleepy to fully grasp what he was saying."

"Can John even use a hammer?"

Kate laughed and shook her head. "I'm not sure, but I think he was feeling a bit 'out-butched' with all my boat building. He was clearly needing some 'man time.'"

They were silent for a moment, enjoying the quiet. The water's surface was so glassy that it looked more like a large lake than the Gulf of Mexico. A light breeze, scented with salt, stirred Ida's hair.

"Kate, I'm going home."

"What?" Kate exclaimed with surprise.

"I've been homesick for a while now. You and John are settled and happy. I want to go home." Ida paused, tilting her head to meet Kate's concerned gaze. "I can go back now and not worry about you."

"But I might worry about you. I don't want you traveling alone. It's too far, Ida."

"I feel so special when you worry about me."

"Don't make fun of me. You know I'll worry about you." Kate gave Ida her best *I'm serious* look.

"Well, don't."

"Are you sure?"

"I'm sure. It's what I want." Ida fussed affectionately with the collar of Kate's shirt. "I miss my brother, and I haven't seen my niece in more than a year. I'm sure she looks like an entirely different person by now. I don't want her to grow up not knowing her aunt."

"Promise me you won't travel alone. I'm serious. I won't let you leave if you do."

Ida smiled at Kate's old habit of looking after her. They'd been best friends since they were kids. Despite her admonishment for Kate not to worry about her, she knew if their situation were reversed she'd be just as concerned for Kate. Caretaking, for Ida, was as much a part of her DNA as blond hair and blue eyes. Ida was the caretaker and Kate was the adventurer. They would have made a perfect match if Kate had developed any romantic interest in women, but she never did.

"There's a family heading north and then east to Alabama. I've already worked it out to travel with them. Don't worry about me, okay? I'm going to be fine. And so are you."

Ida had made the journey from North Georgia to Southern Mississippi with John and Kate over a year ago. They'd headed south about a month after Ida's mother died. It had fallen to Ida to care for her mother in the last year of her life, which she did without regret. Her brother Samuel had a wife and a daughter, and in their father's absence, the entire farm to run while Ida was left to tend their mother.

The necessity of caring for her mother also gave Ida an easy out from a stagnant relationship. She and Chris had struggled for months, maybe longer, before Ida used the excuse of her mother's illness to make the break official. Chris fought the decision, attempting to block the breakup or at the very least, control it, as she tried to control everything else in their relationship. Ida felt as if she had lost her identity while they'd been together and she desperately wanted to find herself again. The decision to leave Chris and care for her mother probably seemed like a sacrifice to an outsider, but it wasn't.

Ida loved her mother dearly, but witnessing the end of her life only cast in stark relief the fact that Ida had settled for less in hers. The bottom line was Ida wasn't happy. So when the offer from Kate and John came to travel south, she jumped at it.

In hindsight, Ida knew she'd left because she badly needed a change of scenery. She needed an escape from the familiar and some distance from a house that was a reminder of the sadness of her mother's passing. But once she'd been clear of all of that for several months, she began to long for home. Not for the life she'd had with Chris. That was most certainly over. But she longed for her childhood home in the foothills of the Blue Mountains.

"I'm guessing we'll both worry about each other. Old habits are hard to change." Kate pulled Ida into a hug. "If you're sure you have to go, then I guess I'll let you. I'll miss you."

"I'll miss you, too." Ida released Kate from their embrace to hold her at arm's length. "I think I'm attached to the Blue Mountains the way you are attached to the sea."

Ida felt sadness, but she knew she was making the right decision. For weeks, Ida had been suffering homesickness but hadn't talked about it with Kate and John because she knew they'd feel bad about having brought her with them. She yearned for the farm her family occupied in the foothills. If a place could be sacred, Ida felt that the Blue Mountains fit that description, at least for her. She felt the absence of place like the loss of a loved one.

CHAPTER THREE

Vivian tended to the horse while Anders unhitched the wagon. After unloading the hay near the back of the barn, they both sauntered over to the long one-story bunk house for their evening meal. Vivian was last to receive a heaping ladle of beans and potatoes next to her cornbread. Eugenia lingered for a moment, her plump hip almost brushing against Vivian's arm. Vivian looked up to meet her glare, at which point Eugenia leaned in and spoke in a hushed voice, "You better watch yourself."

Vivian gave her a confused look. "What are you going on about?"

"I saw Miss Elizabeth coming out of your bunk room earlier. You best be careful." She paused for emphasis. "That one is trouble. Don't you doubt it for a red-hot minute."

Vivian regarded Eugenia's hand, the color of chocolate, still holding the ladle as the large pot rested on the plank table nearby. It was true, Vivian had felt cautious about any interaction with Elizabeth, but she couldn't identify why, so she ignored it.

"And her brother is trouble of a different kind. He don't really like anyone with color, and if he finds out you and Miss Elizabeth have something going on, well, you just better watch your back."

Vivian gave a sweeping glance toward the other men digging into their food as if it was their last meal. They seemed to be ignoring the conversation. "If he doesn't like us because of our color then why did he hire us?" Vivian asked.

Eugenia veered closer. "He don't have no problem having you do work that he don't want to do, or that he thinks is beneath his station. But it'll be a different story if he catches you with Miss Elizabeth. Trust my words when I tell you that."

Vivian just nodded as Eugenia moved with the pot back toward the kitchen. Eugenia had always been kind to Vivian. She had added extra food to Vivian's plate when she'd first arrived probably looking like a walking skeleton. She knew Eugenia would have no other reason to say something to her about Elizabeth and her brother except out of genuine concern. And now she wondered what Elizabeth had been doing in her room. *How does she even know which room belongs to me?*

Vivian ate the rest of her meal in silence. As some of the men settled back into their seats to smoke, she left and walked down the long porch toward her meager quarters. Vivian didn't know what to expect when she opened the door. But in the sparsely set room, she noticed the new things right away.

In the center of her bed lay a pair of new socks.

Elizabeth had brought her socks. That might have been the grandest act of kindness she'd received since she'd left Oklahoma, maybe even before that. Vivian smiled as she remembered their afternoon together. Elizabeth had been surprisingly aggressive in bed. If Vivian had tried to guess at Elizabeth's preferences she'd have been wrong. Once again, Vivian was reminded that she had a lot to learn about women.

Vivian poured water from a nearby pitcher into the bucket on the small table near her narrow bed and began to wash up. She put on her only clean shirt and her new socks before heading out for a walk. She tried her best to foster an air of nonchalance as she left the bunkhouse, but inside she was in a knot of excitement, hoping she'd bump into Elizabeth. Maybe she did manage a calm exterior, but as thoughts of sex with Elizabeth traveled to the front of her mind, her insides began to churn.

Eugenia is right. What are you doing? This has nowhere to go. But why not enjoy it while it lasts?

Vivian marveled at her own feeble circular logic as she climbed a slight rise crowned by a grand old oak. The tree had such immense girth that Elizabeth was shielded from view until Vivian almost stepped on her. She was seated on a blanket with her back against the oak's trunk, facing a flaming sunset made more vivid by the heat rising from the dry earth between the tree and the distant horizon line.

"Hi. Imagine meeting you here."

"I'm just lucky, I guess." Vivian smiled, pleased that her evening was likely about to take a pleasant turn. "Thank you for the socks."

"You're welcome. Would you like to sit? There's plenty of room." Elizabeth patted the empty space next to her on the plaid wool blanket.

Vivian took a seat next to her, but rather than face the sunset she looked at Elizabeth.

"You don't want to watch the sun set?"

"Sunsets happen every day. I'd rather look at you." Elizabeth smiled at the compliment.

Vivian nearly jumped when Elizabeth touched her thigh and moved her fingers slowly across the rough heavyweight fabric of her pants.

"Elizabeth, I—" Eugenia's words of warning briefly rose to the surface then flamed out as quick as a shooting star when Elizabeth's hand stroked her leg. Elizabeth's hand had drifted dangerously up Vivian's tightly clenched thigh.

"Were you about to say something?" Elizabeth asked barely above a whisper.

"Uh, no." Vivian's head began to feel fuzzy. Her hormones were leading her about like a trained pony and Elizabeth clearly held the reins.

It was as if two voices had separated inside Vivian's head and were having a moral debate about the prudence of this particular sexual encounter. One voice echoed Eugenia's caution. The other pressed Vivian to enjoy the moment.

The sun had dropped out of sight although its heat lingered in the darkening evening air. A slight breeze stirred the tall dry grass around them, and the rising quarter moon cast a low glow that made Elizabeth's pale hands look almost ghostly as they moved over Vivian's skin and through her now open shirt. Elizabeth pushed gently against the center of her chest.

"Lie back, Vivian," Elizabeth said.

Vivian's flesh tingled beneath her touch.

CHAPTER FOUR

Ida increased the pace of her gait so that she could catch up with Emily Franklin. Emily had a mane of dark wavy hair that fell just past her shoulders, skin the color of sweet caramel, and dark brown eyes. The moment she'd laid eyes on her, Ida thought she was strikingly beautiful. She seemed young to have two children already.

The Franklins, Emily and Roy, had two daughters, a horse, a cow, and a wagon full of household goods. Plus Stanley Ebbs, who was traveling with them in hopes of staying on to help work their farm once they arrived at their destination. The group created a small caravan. Roy had called it "safety in numbers," and Ida agreed with him. Mostly, the roads were benign, but not always, and it was a bit more intimidating to anyone considering orchestrating an ambush if there was a group to confront rather than a single nomad.

Emily turned and smiled as Ida caught up to her. "Hey."

"Hello. Do you mind if I walk with you for a while?"

"I'd love the company. Good conversation makes all this walking a bit more bearable, don't you think?"

"Absolutely." Ida nodded as she allowed her stride to match Emily's. "Where are you from, Emily?"

"Originally, Baton Rouge. It's on the coast. Have you been there?"

"No, I've never been to Louisiana."

Ida knew from her childhood geography books that Louisiana had at one time extended much farther south, but the water-lying parts of the state, along with New Orleans, had long since been swallowed up by the rising Gulf. The cobblestones of the Crescent City had not been seen since the last category five hurricane washed over its levees over a hundred years ago. New Orleans was not a well-off city. As a result, when the wealthy rose from the ground to the cloud cities that now hovered over the open seas, New Orleans was left to sink.

Most of the large Southern urban areas had been lost in the exodus of the wealthy. Only Houston and Miami had risen when everything collapsed. Jackson, Atlanta, Memphis, Mobile—had all been left to decay and decline, their city centers abandoned for open rural spaces where food could actually be grown. The buildings and trappings of urban life were left deserted to be reclaimed by the elements. Cloud cities, to most folks, seemed so farfetched. Their contrast to life on the ground was unimaginable.

As she looked up to study the sun's position in the sky, Ida found herself wishing she'd worn one of her dresses rather than slacks. If it was this hot already, by noon the temperature and humidity were going to be oppressive.

Roy caught up to them and quickly began to pass them with his longer legs. "Hello, ladies. Just give a shout if you need a break."

"Thanks, honey. We will," Emily said.

They watched Roy as he drew up alongside the wagon and checked on his two young daughters. One of the girls reached for him with outstretched arms. He easily hoisted her out of the buckboard and swung her to the ground so that she could run along with the wagon.

"I wish I had that much energy." Ida adjusted the large satchel she was carrying, shifting the wide leather strap from one shoulder to the other. "How long will it take us to get to Meridian, do you think?"

"Roy estimated three and half days if we make good time. I suspect we'll head north to the main road that runs between Natchez and Meridian and then head east."

"I wasn't sure because when I made this trip before, the group I was traveling with came by a different route." Ida was regretting that she hadn't asked John to draw her a map before she'd left McComb. Being too trusting was one of her faults, and now she realized she was placing her trust in Roy Franklin to know where he was going.

CHAPTER FIVE

Vivian was feeling restless. She was now way past the point at which she'd expected to be back on her eastward trek. If she waited too long to leave she'd be finishing the journey into the mountains after the snow started, and she knew that would make surviving on the trail much tougher.

Vivian was slowly herding a small group of cattle, moving them toward water, when she pondered her situation. She was beginning to chafe under Walt's ever-critical command. He was not someone that she looked up to or respected in the least, so the thought that he controlled her day-to-day existence on the ranch was becoming hard to tolerate. The only element of her life on the ranch that tempered her anger was Elizabeth, but even that was wearing paper thin.

The livestock hit a dry patch, and their movement stirred a powerful dust cloud behind them. Vivian pulled her handkerchief up over her mouth and nose, then dropped back a ways. She allowed her mind to wander to the previous evening when Elizabeth had paid her a late-night visit. There had been several stolen kisses since their meeting at the oak, and then Elizabeth had shown up at Vivian's door wearing nothing but a thin nightgown. They had spent the night together, and Elizabeth slipped out just before dawn, not wanting anyone to see her leaving Vivian's room. The fact that Elizabeth was sneaking around and not open about their time together was a little upsetting. It was also unsettling that each encounter had been on Elizabeth's terms and schedule. The balance of power in their relationship, if you could even call it that, was obviously not in Vivian's favor.

Vivian checked the sun's position in the sky to gauge the time. Her best guess was two o'clock. She moved forward, prodding the lazy animals with a rod to get them to increase their speed. Today they were branding the calves. The sooner that task was over, the sooner she could end her day and turn in.

Walt had seemed on edge the past couple of days, even worse than usual. Vivian knew Walt wasn't stupid and had probably figured out something was going on between Vivian and his sister. He seemed more short-tempered, and in his eyes Vivian could do nothing right. Whether it was spreading hay in the stalls, grooming the horses, or cleaning tack, she had barely been able to keep herself from not responding to his angry retort after angry retort. She was attempting to keep it together until she had at least one more chance to be alone with Elizabeth. But she wouldn't put up with Walt's ill temper forever.

Vivian had just closed the gate, corralling the cattle that were to be branded, when she heard Elizabeth's voice. She was talking to Walt several yards away near the barn. As Vivian walked toward them, Elizabeth's body language told her something was off. Elizabeth turned and looked at her as if she didn't know who she was. That should have been Vivian's clue to walk away, but she didn't. As she drew closer, Elizabeth spoke to her in a clipped voice.

"I left some things in the back of the wagon over there. Take them to Eugenia."

No please. No hello. No acknowledgment that just the previous night, she had been in Vivian's bed begging her not to stop moving her tongue over very sensitive places.

In addition to her hesitation to respond to Elizabeth's command, there had to have been a look of disbelief on Vivian's face, because that was how she felt. Even still, Elizabeth's demeanor didn't shift. Her glance was cold, and her body language remained reserved and distant. Vivian must have stood staring longer than she realized because she felt a shove at her shoulder.

"Are you deaf? She gave you a direct command." Walt had

pushed her and stepped toward her as if he was going to do it again. Elizabeth stood motionless, her arms crossed in front of her chest. "Oh, did you think because she used you for sex that you mean anything to her? Or that she won't treat you like the hired hand you are?" Walt's tone was acerbic and his words slammed into Vivian's chest as if she'd been struck by a heavy stone.

Obviously, he knew they'd been sleeping together so why was Elizabeth sneaking around? Unless clandestine encounters were part of what made it exciting for her. Vivian thought she was already jaded by how poorly people generally treated one another. She'd seen enough in her life in Oklahoma to know more than a few individuals were predatory in nature. Yet this revelation about Elizabeth shocked her. Vivian felt sick and then she felt rage.

Elizabeth must have seen the shift because her expression changed just barely, almost as if she were seeing Vivian for the first time. Vivian didn't wait for another word to be uttered. She walked to the wagon, hefted the wooden crate of food supplies, and carried it to the kitchen at the rear of the bunkhouse. She didn't look back.

By late afternoon, Anders, another ranch hand named Simms, and Vivian were in the small pen closest to the barn branding some calves when Walt came to stand near the fence to watch. It was past the hottest hours of the day. The shadows were long across the pen from the low altitude of the sun, and dust was thick in the air as each calf struggled to move away from the branding iron when its turn arrived. After each calf was marked, the iron was placed back in the coals. Vivian wanted to keep it hot so that the whole process could be as quick as possible for the calf. She hated this task with a passion. In this desolate place was it really necessary to scar the calves with a brand that no one would see or care about? Brands didn't keep desperate, starving people from stealing a steer. This was an ineffective exercise in ownership. Vivian felt it was all ego on Walt Hudson's part, too, and for every burn to hide she inflicted, the anger and discontent in her chest grew. But they weren't her cattle, and this wasn't her ranch, and after one more hot meal, she was leaving. She'd had all she could take of the Hudson family.

Only two calves remained in the holding pen when Walt

stepped through the gate and walked toward them. Something about the way Vivian was handling this chore displeased him. She could tell by the strain of his jaw as he approached.

"You're not holding it on the hide long enough," Walt barked loudly. Simms and Anders had already roped the animal's legs and pulled him down on his side. Walt took the branding iron from Vivian and aimed it at the calf's hindquarters. He held it to the flesh for what seemed like an eternity as the calf writhed and wailed.

"Enough!" Vivian grabbed Walt's arm and pulled it away from the calf's smoking flank. "There's no need to torture the poor animal just so you can mark him. You're inflicting a wound that's too deep."

Walt was seething. "Don't fucking tell me how to brand my cattle, half-breed."

"What did you just call me?"

Simms and Anders released the squealing calf and stepped aside.

"I called you what you are, a fucking half-breed," said Walt before spitting on her boots. By the time he looked up Vivian had toppled him. She punched him twice in the face before he could react. By the time he was able to shove her backward into the dirt he had blood streaming from his nose. Then they were both back on their feet, fists raised and clenched, ready to strike again. Walt swung high and Vivian dodged, landing a punch in Walt's ribs. But she didn't pull back soon enough, and he got an elbow to her jaw, sending her reeling backward.

"You're off this ranch, Yates!" Walt smeared blood away from his nose with the back of his hand.

"You're an asshole, Walt. I should have left weeks ago."

The standoff was drawing a crowd now as the two remaining men that worked the ranch came to stand just outside the split-rail fence. Walt and Vivian's dislike of each other had been building for weeks, and now it erupted. Walt and Vivian lunged at each other. Walt had Vivian around the neck and pummeled her stomach, knocking the wind out of her. She gasped and dropped to her knees. Where she had the advantage over Walt in height and agility, he had the advantage in muscle mass. Every punch he landed seemed to carry more weight and do more damage. But she had righteous anger on her side, which spiked her adrenaline.

Vivian grabbed Walt by the shirt and put her full weight into shoving him onto his back. As she sat, pinning him to the ground, she repeatedly punched his face. Vivian was so distracted by her furor that she didn't see Elizabeth until it was too late. She felt the heat before she saw the sizzling red-hot branding iron aimed in her direction as Elizabeth lunged at her. In an effort to avoid contact, Vivian toppled off Walt and scrambled to get out of Elizabeth's path. She almost made it, but scuttling backward, she was unable to fully get to her feet. She tried to block the next strike, managing to capture Elizabeth's arm, but not before the hot iron seared through her shirt. The glowing metal only touched her skin for the briefest second before Vivian deflected Elizabeth's forward motion. Even that slight contact sent a wave of shock and nausea washing over her. Vivian cried out. She had the vague recognition of someone screaming as she recoiled. She rolled onto her side, then struggled to her feet, staggering away from Elizabeth.

It was Elizabeth who was screaming. "How dare you strike my brother! How dare you! Who do you think you are?"

Elizabeth put herself between Vivian and Walt, who now sat in the dust, blinking as if he'd just been released from some moment of demon possession. He looked at the branding iron in his sister's hand with a stunned expression on his bloodied face.

As Vivian reached the rail fence at the edge of the enclosure, she dropped to her knees, leaning against the lowest boards for support. She was breathing hard and still feeling sick.

"Get up, Vivian!" Elizabeth tossed the branding iron toward the fire pit and bent down to reach for Vivian's arm.

"Don't touch me!"

Elizabeth looked around the pen at the four other men who had stood silently watching the altercation. Walt got to his feet with an air of bewilderment.

"She started it and I would have finished it. I didn't need your help." He spat in the dry dirt for emphasis, before seeming to notice the men standing nearby. "Everybody get back to work! The show's over!" he shouted as he strode out of the enclosure.

Vivian was on her knees with her forehead in the dirt, trying to calm the nausea that kept rising from the excruciating pain in her chest. Her shirt was burned and her chest underneath felt badly blistered.

Elizabeth loomed over her. "Vivian, I said get up." She placed her hand on Vivian's forearm as if she meant to pull her to her feet.

"Get away from me!" Vivian jerked her arm away and willed herself to get up. She got to an unstable standing position, her vision blurry from tears, and walked toward her bunk. After a moment, she heard footsteps following her.

Once inside, Vivian leaned against the small table where she kept her bucket of water. Her eyes were closed and she was trying to steady her shallow breathing. She'd never experienced anything that hurt as badly as the branding iron she'd just encountered. Vivian wet a clean rag and tentatively placed the cool damp cloth over the burn. The sensation of touching the scorched flesh made her stomach pitch and roll. She bent over to keep herself from passing out.

"Let me see." Elizabeth's words sounded like a command rather than a request.

"Who are you? I don't even know you."

"I know you're angry with me, but I did that for your own good." Elizabeth reached for Vivian's hand where she'd braced it on the table.

"Don't." Vivian glared at Elizabeth and turned her back toward her as she slowly removed the ruined shirt. She reached for another shirt draped over the only stiff-backed wooden chair in the room, and turned to regard Elizabeth as she worked with shaky fingers at the buttons.

"I'm leaving," Vivian said.

"When?"

"Now."

Before Vivian could say more, there was a soft knock and Eugenia stuck her head through the slightly ajar door. Eugenia regarded the scene without the slightest hint of surprise on her face. She had a bulging cloth sack in her hand.

"Anders told me what happened. I brought you what I could spare. Here's some salted beef, some corn cakes, and a few potatoes."

Vivian nodded. "Thanks."

"You take care of yourself, Vivian Yates," said Eugenia. She placed the sack of provisions on the bed and gave Elizabeth a direct glare that seethed *you should be ashamed of yourself* before she left.

"You aren't leaving tonight."

"What did you say?" Vivian turned to face Elizabeth as she finished buttoning the last buttons on her shirt.

"You'll do what I say, when I say it." Elizabeth regarded Vivian coldly.

"You don't own me. I'll do as I please, and at the moment that means leaving."

"You can't leave. You've got nothing and no one," said Elizabeth with sheer condescension.

Vivian felt the hurt of Elizabeth's words as if she'd been struck again with the iron, but she didn't respond. What could she say? She felt used, dismissed, hurt, and all of it at the hands of someone she thought actually cared about her.

"So that's it then? You fuck me and then leave like it means nothing?" Elizabeth stood defiantly between Vivian and the door, her arms across her chest.

"Clearly, it meant nothing to you. And now you can go fuck yourself, literally."

Vivian had hardly gotten the words out of her mouth before Elizabeth slapped her hard across her face. The blow caught Vivian off guard. She glared at Elizabeth through the strands of hair that had fallen across her face from the blow.

"I'll always be under your skin now, Vivian. You'll never forget me, I've seen to that."

Rage surged in Vivian's chest, rivaling the heat she felt from the burn.

She needed to get the hell off the Hudson Ranch. She saw the furious, arrogant look on Elizabeth's face and realized she had no idea who this woman was or what she was capable of. They'd had a fling and it was over. It wasn't as if it hadn't been obvious to her on some level that Elizabeth was just toying with her, but she never anticipated this level of viciousness. In all honesty, they had both used each other. That was that. Vivian didn't want any attachments and she didn't need any attachments. She didn't have anyone and she didn't *need* anyone.

After a moment of silence, Vivian moved about her small quarters, placing her sparse belongings into a leather bag. She stowed the food that Eugenia had brought. She rolled the blanket from the foot of her bunk and tied it to the outside of the bag. Elizabeth stood silently by as she watched Vivian retrieve her bow and a small quiver of arrows, the last two items she strapped to the side of the leather pack. She slung the bag over her shoulder, holding her hat in her hand.

Vivian worked the muscles of her clenched jaw. She wanted to say something to Elizabeth, but what? Nothing seemed worth saying at this point. After a long moment, she lowered her gaze from Elizabeth's face to the floor, pulled on her hat, and walked through the door, leaving Elizabeth standing by herself in the center of the small room.

"You'll regret this, Vivian Yates!"

Vivian didn't respond. As she passed the woodpile at the edge of the small toolshed, she pulled a hatchet from a wedge of wood, and without looking back strode purposefully toward the road and headed east, away from the now setting sun.

❖

Vivian walked most of the night. She was far too angry to sit or sleep. Her heart pounded with rage at her own stupidity. Her chest felt so tight that her body registered the stiff seismic impact of every footfall. She had stayed too long. Long enough to care about Elizabeth, and long enough to be hurt by her. The burn ached, but no more intensely than the wound in her heart. Vivian had thought

Walt was a narrow-minded bully, but he was nothing compared to the wrath his sister wrought.

At one point, she opened the front of her shirt to allow the cool night air to sweep across the injury to her chest. The constant brush of the shirt fabric as she walked was irritating the now darkening "H" over her breast. She paused her furious march long enough to unbutton her shirt and pull the thin cotton fabric to the side. As she worked the buttons free, she looked up and realized the moon was full. She noted to herself that she would see the moon disappear and return to fullness again before she was within striking distance of the Blue Mountains.

CHAPTER SIX

The steady cadence of the horses' hooves and the creaking of the wagon wheels on the hard dirt path was the only noise Ida could hear as their small group passed through the pine forests of South Central Mississippi. Perfectly straight and tall long-leaf pines anchored in sandy soil stretched as far as she could see. Old government-managed state delineations had long since disappeared, but general areas and regions still carried their former names. Even before everything went dark and the central government collapsed, the country had broken into small autonomous units as life became more intensely localized. Those units still carried most of the old names.

The path they walked had once been a major highway, but now it was a wagon trail and a footpath. Occasionally, they came across black rocks that were the remnants of the once paved surface that had since been broken apart by water, earth, and weeds and further covered over by organic matter.

It had been more than one hundred years since planet Earth reached peak oil. One percent of the Earth's population, the wealthiest individuals of the world, rose above the chaos, literally, that erupted when the seas crested after oil's demise. Enormous cloud cities were constructed to insulate the elite from the collapse they had contributed to on the ground. New York, Toronto, London, Stockholm, Houston, Miami, Hong Kong, Monaco, Rome, and other metropolises now floated above it all, among the clouds. Those that remained on the ground lived on the land that remained after the coastlines moved inland. Their world on the ground was reminiscent of a nineteenth-century existence where running water, central air and heat, electricity, cars, and supermarkets were now the stuff of folklore.

Traveling to the Gulf Coast had been an epic endeavor for Ida. Up to that point, she'd never been outside the territorial border of Georgia. When she'd made the journey south to the Gulf, she'd had the company of Kate and John. Ida had never done anything remotely this adventurous alone. She and Kate had been constant companions since childhood. Upon reflection, she realized it was probably good for her to strike out on her own to prove to herself that she could do it. To prove to herself that she wasn't afraid.

Late in the day, they came upon the charred remains of conifers, silent markers to some catastrophic event.

"Probably started by lightning." Stanley, Roy's hired man, stopped beside Ida in the roadbed to examine the destruction. "Looks like it didn't spread too far. I guess rain must have started soon after the strike and drowned it out."

Without further comment, Stanley turned and walked on ahead.

Lightning was a real threat. With the slight rise in global temperature, the frequency and severity of lightning storms had increased. She didn't understand the science behind it, but there was no doubting the reality of its destructive force. Less water and more fire were modern-day realities. Ida lingered for a moment trying to reimagine the scene. The smell of burnt wood still lingered in the air. She had a healthy respect for fire. In truth, she was a little afraid of it, having witnessed how quickly a flame could spread. Once she and her brother, Samuel, had witnessed a brush fire near the back of the house, and before they could extinguish it, half the yard was scorched, the house itself blackened by the closeness of the blaze.

Ida was lost in thought when she realized Stanley was back at her side. "Some riders are headed our way."

Ida strained to look around the wagon to the road ahead. She saw two figures on horseback moving in their direction. Stanley was a lean, thinly muscled man, probably stronger than he looked, but not the most intimidating fellow. He had a thick wooden rod in one hand and a large hunting knife in a leather sheath at his waist. His demeanor seemed tense as he watched the travelers on horseback approach.

"Maybe you should climb into the wagon, Ms. Ida."

Ida nodded and accepted Stanley's hand as he helped her climb up into the wooden shell of the wagon with Emily and the two girls.

"What's going on?" Emily asked.

"Some riders are coming. I think Stanley and Roy want us to stay out of sight for a bit."

It annoyed Ida that she needed to seek protection in the wagon at the slightest threat. She carried a good-natured grudge against her father because he never helped or encouraged her to learn how to defend herself in a threatening situation. She vowed that when she returned home she was going to make her brother teach her to shoot a bow and maybe even use a knife. At the very least he could give her some tips. Ida wasn't really angry with her father, but because she was more feminine in manner, his old-fashioned ideas had relegated her to the role of one who required protection rather than someone who could defend herself. Her friend Kate had been much more of a tomboy growing, up so she had learned to hunt and use a bow right alongside her brothers. Ida was sometimes envious of the equality that Kate enjoyed as a teen.

The sound of hooves on the hard-packed ground brought Ida's attention back to the present. There was a canvas opening at the back of the wagon that allowed her to see who was approaching. A man leaned sideways in his saddle and tried to peer past the slit of the wagon cover. As he did, Ida leaned farther into the shadows of the wagon's interior, but not before she saw certain details of his face. His skin was prickled with a small growth of beard, and he had a scar from his temple all the way to his jaw on the right side of his face. Ida knew she would not soon forget the man's features or the dark anger that emanated from his menacingly shadowed eyes.

CHAPTER SEVEN

A little more than two days into her journey, Vivian crossed the Kisatchie Forest. The understory was thick with ferns and the pines were mixed with hardwoods and cypress. Even the air smelled different. It hung heavy with the heat-baked scent of plant decay. Luckily, the dirt path she'd been following was still clearly etched out of the surrounding greenery. It was an easy path to follow. Occasionally, a small swampy pond would appear near the path, its water black from tannic acid. The dark water was safe to drink, but it had an odd, bitter taste. Vivian was hopeful she'd find a better water source soon.

During one of her breaks, Vivian pulled out a tattered, yellowed map. She unfolded the weathered document and spread it out on the ground. The map had belonged to her grandfather. Over the years, he'd asked travelers about details of this region and then he'd made notations. It had taken him years to compile all the particulars. He had planned to make this trip at some point in his life. Of course, all the notations were based on rumor and secondhand information. Her granddad never made it this far.

I guess I'll know in a few days how accurate it is. If his figuring was correct, there should be a good-sized shallow lake at the halfway point between Carthage and Natchez. She hoped that was true. Vivian refolded the map and tucked it gently into a pocket inside her leather bag. She stood, resettled her hat, and headed east.

It felt simultaneously eerie and reassuring to walk through so much wooded land without encountering another human. All the earth seemed quiet but at the same time very alive. Birds, moths, and even a few snakes silently crossed Vivian's path as she marched deeper into the Kisatchie wilderness.

The pathway narrowed through a particularly thick grove of broad-leafed shrubs and sumac when something off to the south caught Vivian's eye. Curiosity got the best of her, as it usually did, and she veered off the trail to peer into a grove of cypress. Now completely encircled in greenery, Vivian saw the origin of the glint that inspired her to change course: a line of steel skeletal remains. Cars, as if stranded in some century-old traffic jam, were barely discernible above their vine-covered resting place.

Vivian moved closer to brush some of the creepers aside and scan inside one of the relic's former windows. She tried to imagine what it must have been like to live in a time when motorized transportation was readily available. She'd read in books how in past centuries almost everyone had a car, sometimes more than one. Now in the face of depleted energy resources, this opulence seemed like publicly sanctioned insanity.

The abuse, dependence, and ultimate waste of the Earth's fossil fuels had fostered the populations of centuries past to egregiously exceed the carrying capacity of the planet in every respect, until the planet literally seemed to collapse under the pressure of it all. And then Mother Nature joined in the fun. The last decade of available oil had been preceded by large-scale famine brought on when the climate teetered off its axis. That slight quiver produced a series of late springs and cool summers that resulted in shortened growing cycles, which caused mass food shortages. People suffered and so did their livestock. The weakened population was hit by a flu epidemic that spread rapidly, wiping out entire communities. It was a one-two-three punch that the world barely survived. And in truth, what endured looked quite different. The population had been greatly reduced and everything became extremely localized. Those who could grow their own food and owned land to do so fared the best. Communities that were the most self-sustaining remained even today.

Vivian ran her fingers over a small patch of an exposed auto hood, now rusted and rough from the humid air. Shards of brown flaked off onto her fingertips, staining her skin. As she stood looking down at the remains of derelict excess, her grandfather's words came to her. *Man did not weave the web of life; he is merely a strand in it. What he does to the web, he does to himself.*

❖

Several days into her trek, Vivian came across a large, shallow, freshwater lake. On her hand-drawn map, the body of water had been given the name Catahoula. So far, the map had been fairly accurate, which led her to calculate that she was probably only three days from Natchez and the crossing of the great Mississippi River. The success or failure of that crossing would bear her forward into Alabama territory or abruptly end her journey.

By early afternoon on the third day after leaving the lake, she began to see clear signs that she was getting near the Mississippi. The vegetation grew lushly, as it was prone to do near ample water. Vivian walked past a few homesteads set way back off the roadway and passed a couple of travelers without incident, one on foot and one on horseback. As she drew closer to the massive river, the remnants of old stone pylons stood side by side like ancient rock sentinels from a time before now, marking the spot where a bridge had once been anchored. Vivian stopped near the stones, which were on a bit of a rise above the water line, and surveyed the wide expanse. Swift-moving brown water swirled beneath her as she stood on the high bank surveying the massive waterway. Looking north and south, the river cut a broad liquid channel across the landscape as far as she could see. The churning torrent demanded respect, adoration even, as it continued its unchallenged southward journey to the Gulf. The ferry lines were visible below, running from one side of the river to the other. She could see a ferryboat returning from the eastern bank as she studied the vista spread out in front of her.

Clearly, Natchez was a booming settlement. From where Vivian stood on the opposite bank, she could see horses pulling carriages loaded with goods, wood-sided buildings, stone buildings, and more people milling about than she had probably ever seen in one place. It dawned on her that she would probably not be able to cross this river by ferry without striking some sort of bartering deal. And she didn't really have anything she could part with. She'd already stripped down her belongings to the bare minimum when she'd set out from Oklahoma. Somehow in her figuring she'd neglected to consider the need to barter passage. Somewhere in the back of her mind, she had imagined just being able to swim across the river. But now that she was at its edge, she realized swimming wouldn't be an option. She'd already seen two alligators ease themselves from a sunny spot on the bank into the muddy water, and based on the tension working against the side of the ferry, there was also quite a strong current.

As she stepped up on the plank landing, Vivian felt dwarfed by the wide expanse of dark water. It was almost as if she felt the weight and power of it deep in her chest. Only one other traveler waited for passage nearby. He had a mule loaded with goods. Sacks and boxes were tied all around the pack animal, which stood silently, shifting from foot to foot. Vivian fell in beside the man and waited for the ferry master to return. In her palm she held the short wooden handle of the axe she'd lifted from the Hudson Ranch. She was prepared to let it go in return for safe passage. *One less remnant by which to remember the Hudson place is a good thing.*

CHAPTER EIGHT

According to Vivian's map, after crossing the region between Natchez and Meridian she would pass through the southern boundary of the Bienville Wilderness and end up near Bonita Lake, just past the village boundary of Meridian. The wide, rutted dirt trail ran straight, like a line of twine strung between two sticks, through thick groves of long leaf pines with sandy floors. The heat of late July was relentless. It hung around her like a copious damp cloud from early morning to late evening. She built small fires at night for cooking and to smoke the bugs away, but could hardly stand to be near the heat of the flames.

A few days into her trek through the flatland pine forests, she came upon several mammoth earthen mounds. Fire ants with nothing but time to dig and build had constructed these huge, dried clay domes for themselves. Vivian gave them a wide berth.

Each day, cicadas sang in the heat like huge symphonies of tiny high-pitched violins. They seemed to crescendo as the temperature climbed toward its peak every afternoon.

Late in the afternoon on the fourth day after leaving Natchez, Vivian came upon a small group camped just off the road. She saw the thin thread of smoke from their cook fire, and as she drew closer she could see that they had a covered wagon, a couple of horses, a cow, and what looked like several members of a family. After traveling alone for so long, Vivian thought it might be nice to have a little company for one night. From the looks of things, they seemed like a non-threatening group so she approached, albeit cautiously, to find out if they would share their fire. Vivian had killed a rabbit not too far back up the road, so she at least had something to contribute to the evening meal if they were inclined to include her. One of the men stood as she got near. He moved out in front of the group a little ways to meet her.

"Hello, there." Vivian stopped several feet from the man.

"Hi, yourself." The man extended his hand in greeting. "I'm Roy."

"Vivian." She gave his hand a firm shake. He seemed friendly enough. "I was wondering if you'd mind if I camped near your group for the night. I have some game I can share." She held up the limp rabbit by its ears.

"You must be a good shot." Roy cocked his head as he studied the sight of entry just through the rabbit's eye socket.

"I can clean him if you like."

"Sounds good. Come, I'll introduce you," said Roy. He motioned for her to follow his lead.

Vivian stepped behind him and moved closer to the small group around the fire. Her gaze came to rest on a beautiful young blond woman who was stirring the pot that hung low over the fire. The woman met her stare with what seemed to be equal curiosity. Vivian realized Roy was talking and tried to redirect her attention with limited success.

"This is Stanley; my wife, Emily; my daughter, Lucy; and this is Ida."

When Roy said the last name, Vivian took special notice that he was pointing to the blonde who had captured her attention.

"My daughter Anne is resting as she's not feeling well."

Vivian nodded to the group.

"My name is Vivian. I'll just go clean this rabbit and we can add it to whatever you've already got for dinner."

She noticed that Ida kept watching her from across the fire pit. So much so that it was making her nervous.

"I'll be right back."

Vivian moved away from the group and eased her pack off and to the ground, laying the rabbit carcass nearby. She'd worn the straps of her bag over both shoulders for the day and was now realizing that had probably been a mistake. Trying to give the burn time to heal, she had mostly carried the leather satchel over her right shoulder, but that was causing serious fatigue so she'd opted to split the load between both shoulders today. The burning sensation over her left breast told her that the wound was definitely aggravated from the friction of the strap. She'd be feeling pain tomorrow for sure.

Vivian moved away from camp to skin and clean the rabbit, then returned with the meat to the fire. Emily and the child had moved closer to the wagon, probably to check on Emily's other daughter. Stanley and Roy were checking out the front wheel of the wagon. The only person who remained by the cook fire was Ida. She smiled at Vivian as she approached.

As Vivian came to stand beside her, Ida reached over and handed her a large cast iron skillet. Vivian pulled her hunting knife free and cut the rabbit into smaller pieces before dropping them into the pan, to which Ida added some lard. Ida took the pan from Vivian and set it into the coals near the pot she'd been stirring. Neither of them spoke during this exchange. Vivian couldn't decide if the silence made her more nervous or less nervous. She studied Ida as she stirred the food and added some salt. She assumed that Ida had no idea how lovely she was; her humble demeanor conveyed as much. She carried the sort of beauty that most women envied. Ida, with her floral-printed shirt buttoned snugly over her supple breasts, sleeves cuffed and rolled to her elbows, and slacks that were tailored just enough to show off her round hips. Her silky blond hair was pulled into a knot so that just a few strands hung along her soft jawline. Ida possessed crystal blue eyes and full pink lips. Like an angel, that was how Vivian would describe her. If Vivian had been some soldier wounded on some ancient battlefield, she would have wanted her field nurse to look like Ida. Hers would be the face to inspire you to fight to survive.

Not only did she find Ida attractive, but Vivian had the strong feeling that they were connected in some way, as if she'd known her in a former life. Whatever the cause, from the moment she'd laid eyes on Ida, she had an aching desire to pull her into her arms and never let her go. The sensation increased Vivian's anxiety as she stood beside Ida as she stirred the food. Vivian decided she needed to sit down and attempt to settle her nerves. She leaned back against a fallen tree that lay along one side of the camp, just a few feet from the fire, and watched Ida cook.

"Do you mind if I sit here?" Vivian finally asked, breaking their silence.

Ida glanced over at Vivian only for a moment as she continued her vigil over the group's supper. "I don't mind." It was all Ida could do to keep her hands from shaking under Vivian's gaze.

When Vivian had first approached the group, Ida was struck by how attractive she was. As Roy had introduced their small gathering, Ida had watched Vivian unabashedly from across the fire pit. She couldn't help but stare at the tall, darkly tanned woman with jet-black hair that hung loosely and casually near her collar, with a few curls turning up near her jawline. She was wearing straight-cut men's trousers with a white shirt that, despite its travel-weary state, was quite striking against her sun-browned skin. Vivian's frame was lean, her pants hung low, just clinging to her hipbones, and when she'd looked directly at Ida across the flames, Ida had felt the depth of her gaze in every nerve ending. Vivian's dark brown eyes held a wildness that intrigued and excited Ida. And now Vivian was seated a few feet away, watching her cook.

"So are you walking by yourself?" asked Ida.

"Yeah. And what about you? How are you connected to this group?"

"I'm—"

Emily interrupted her as she returned to the fire pit. "Ida, I'm sorry I left you with the cooking."

"No problem. How's Anne feeling?"

"She's no better. I'm a little worried that her fever is getting worse." Emily stood next to Ida with her hands on her hips, gazing into the fire as if she were lost in thought.

With Emily standing nearby, Ida felt her unease settle a bit. She wanted to talk more with Vivian, but she also needed to get a better handle on her emotions. Having Emily join her at the fire helped her calm down. They worked together to finish the meal while Vivian looked on from the sidelines. Every time Ida glanced in her direction, Vivian would quickly avert her eyes. The realization that Vivian was as curious about her as she was about Vivian made Ida happy.

As dinner progressed, so did conversation.

"So, Vivian, where are you from?" asked Roy.

"Oklahoma."

"I thought Oklahoma was a desert." Stanley chewed slowly while he waited on the answer. It seemed by his tone that he doubted Vivian's response.

"Most of that territory is a desert. I was living in the lower, southeastern edge. I dropped down through Texas and then cut across." Vivian ate slowly, seeming to carefully choose her words.

"Probably the best route since you'd find more water the farther south you go," said Roy. Stanley could only nod in agreement at Roy's endorsement of Vivian's route.

Ida was listening to the discussion intently in an attempt to gather more information about their handsome dinner guest. Emily rejoined the group after taking some supper to Anne, who was still resting on the platform bed in the back of the wagon.

When Roy saw Emily's face, the subject shifted. "Is she feeling better?"

"I'm afraid not. I think her fever is higher than it was earlier. She wouldn't even try to eat. I'm not sure what else to do."

They hadn't been on the main road for more than a day when the child became ill. Both of the Franklin children were young. They had two girls, one six-year-old and one who was eight. The older started showing signs of sickness the previous night, and by noon, Emily and Roy were concerned. They decided to stop for the day, and if the situation didn't improve, then Roy would consider turning back to Natchez to find a healer.

News of Anne's condition dampened further conversation as everyone sat silently focusing on their food. After a while, the group dispersed to ready the camp for nightfall. Dishes were scraped clean, animals watered, and each retired to their chosen spot to sleep for the night.

Ida had lingered by the fire. Watching the slowly dying flames settled her and helped her relax. She could easily lose herself for some time just staring into the glowing embers. Her mind was miles away on thoughts of home so she didn't hear Vivian walk up behind her until she spoke in a low voice.

"Is that coffee? I wouldn't say no to a cup if you have any to spare."

Startled, Ida looked up from her seated position. Vivian was standing closer than was necessary for Ida to hear the request, and her proximity caused Ida's heart rate to surge.

"I didn't mean to surprise you."

"It's okay. I was just letting my mind drift."

"Pleasant thoughts?"

"Yes," said Ida. She smiled as she poured Vivian a cup of coffee.

Their fingers brushed and Ida was back to being unsettled. She tried to read Vivian's expression but was at a loss. Vivian looked intently at her over the rim of the cup Ida had just handed her.

"Staring at a fire causes my mind to drift, too."

Ida liked the way that Vivian seemed so comfortable in her own skin. She exuded confidence, but not in a showy sort of way. Before Ida could think of anything else to say, Roy walked up with stress evident on his face.

"Anne isn't getting any better. At first light, I think we'll turn back toward Natchez and try to find a healer. Natchez is probably the closest large settlement."

"I'm so sorry," said Ida, reaching out to gently touch Roy's arm. She hadn't known the Franklins long, but she already cared about them. "Is there anything I can do?"

"Thank you, but I don't think so. Emily is sitting up with her. I'll try and get a little sleep so we can leave first thing. Mostly I don't want her sister or anyone else getting sick."

"Maybe it's not something someone can catch." Vivian shifted on her feet as she spoke, sinking her free hand into the front pocket of her trousers.

"I thought that, too. It could be her appendix or something else we can't see," Roy said. "Ida, I'm sorry. I know I promised I'd see you as far as Alabama Territory. You're more than welcome to follow us to Natchez and stay with us until we're on the trail again."

Ida considered Roy's invitation. If indeed little Anne needed some sort of surgery then her condition could get much worse before it got better. The family might be required to stay in Natchez for a while. The last thing Roy and Emily needed was one more person to look after. What were her options? She needed to think this through before making a decision.

"Thank you for being so considerate, Roy. You get some rest and don't worry about me."

Roy nodded and headed toward his family's wagon, now warmly lit by a hanging lantern.

"What are you going to do?" asked Vivian.

"I'd rather keep going. I'm anxious to get home. But I'm not so naïve that I don't realize I might have difficulty by myself." Ida bit her lower lip as she watched the jumping light of the dying campfire.

"We could travel together. Or, what I meant to say is, you could travel with me."

Vivian's voice pulled Ida's from her thoughts. Light from the fire reflected in Vivian's direct gaze.

"What?"

"We're walking in the same direction. If you want to keep going then maybe we could walk together for a while."

"How far are you going?" Ida asked.

"I'm going as far as the Blue Mountains in North Georgia."

"The Blue Mountains? That's where I'm going." Ida looked at Vivian with surprise.

Ida regarded Vivian, trying to read her expression. Vivian shifted under Ida's gaze, and for the first time, Ida noticed that when she shifted and moved her shoulder she seemed to wince. Ida hadn't noticed this earlier when Vivian had first arrived, but she saw it now.

"You're hurt." Ida stepped over so that she could see Vivian's face more clearly.

"No. I'm fine."

"I thought you were hurt just now when I saw you wince as you moved your shoulder. And now I see there's blood on the front of your shirt."

Ida stepped a little closer, and Vivian took a step back. Ida looked into Vivian's face and tried to convey the compassion she was feeling toward this woman she barely knew.

"Sit down and let me take a look."

Vivian hesitated, but did as Ida requested.

Vivian sat cross-legged, leaning forward so that her shirt hung away from her chest. The small dark patches of blood seemed to be in the spot where the leather strap from her shoulder pack would have lain. Ida made a move to open the collar of Vivian's shirt and Vivian jerked back.

"May I see?" asked Ida.

Vivian sighed and leaned forward a little for her inspection. Ida unbuttoned the top two buttons of Vivian's shirt and pulled the cloth open so she could examine her chest. Ida was a little shocked when she saw the angry wound. She examined the singed H and then Vivian's eyes. Ida wanted badly to ask how the burn had happened, but she bit her tongue. Somehow she sensed that even allowing her to see the wound was more than Vivian wanted to reveal, so she didn't ask more.

Ida offered to mix some herbs into a paste that would help soothe the injury. Vivian sat quietly as Ida crushed the plant matter from her supplies into one of the bowls with just a splash of water and a dash of ash from near the fire. She knelt again beside Vivian.

"Hold your shirt open so I can put this on the burn."

Vivian silently complied. She pulled away at Ida's first touch with the cool, green-brown paste. "Sorry," said Vivian. "I flinched."

"It's okay. It must hurt pretty badly. Hopefully, this will help."

"Actually, it was feeling kind of numb, but I think the strap from my bag aggravated it today."

Vivian gave Ida a weak smile, watching her as she gently applied the herbal salve just above Vivian's left breast.

The sensation of touching Vivian's bare skin did nothing to calm Ida's nervous feelings, but she did her best to stay focused on her task as she applied the salve, and not on the alluring flesh she glimpsed. After a moment, Ida rocked back on her heels.

"Okay, that's all I can do for now with limited supplies." She wiped the remaining herbal salve from her fingers onto the loose fabric of her slacks. "Better?"

Vivian buttoned her shirt with a shy expression on her face and responded in a soft voice. "Yeah, thanks."

Ida was puzzled by her own behavior. What was it about Vivian that made her want to treat her as she would, well, as someone she cared about? She hardly knew her. But there was a warmth and soundness about Vivian that drew Ida to her. She would have to riddle more over the magnetic pull that Vivian seemed to wield.

"I think I'm going to turn in." Ida was still kneeling fairly close to Vivian. It was hard to discern if the flushed warmth she was feeling in her cheeks was from the ebbing fire or from Vivian seated next to her.

"Listen, I appreciate the offer for us to travel together. I just want you to know that I won't be upset if you change your mind by morning." Although Ida hoped she wouldn't, she didn't want Vivian to feel any pressure to look out for someone she'd just met.

"I won't change my mind," said Vivian.

The sound of certainty in her voice sent a shiver up Ida's spine.

"Okay, then." Ida stood to make her way to a spot near the wagon where her blanket and bag had been settled. "Until tomorrow."

"Until tomorrow. Good night, Ida."

"Good night, Vivian."

Vivian watched Ida cross the camp and begin to arrange her blanket on the ground near the wagon. Why had she offered to travel with Ida? Wasn't the painful burn on her chest enough of a reminder that she should avoid women? She let out a long sigh as she got to her feet and moved away from the dying fire to set up her bedroll.

Stretched beneath the dark heavens, Vivian tried to relax, but her mind was occupied with thoughts of all that had happened to her since she'd left Oklahoma. What did she hope to find when she reached the Blue Mountains? Could a place, even a sacred place, fill the space in her chest that felt hollow? She hoped so. But more immediately and more urgently, she was resolved to guard her heart from further injury.

She would allow herself to seek companionship. But she would set boundaries that no one would be allowed to cross. This would be the only way to ensure that others had no control over her happiness. She alone would control how close she allowed anyone to get. She would not allow herself to be ambushed by betrayal again. Ever.

She looked over to where Ida had settled in. Even camped so near others she felt utterly alone. At this moment, she knew she was a stranger even to herself. She hoped reaching the Blue Mountains would help her find her true self again. As she rolled onto her back to gaze up at the stars, she fought the urge to cry. Feeling sorry for herself would solve nothing. She made her own way in the world. She was tied to no one and nothing except the goal of reaching the mountains. Not everyone had the freedom she enjoyed, and she tried to rally positive thoughts around that notion as she willed herself to sleep.

CHAPTER NINE

As they stood in the roadway watching the Franklins depart, Ida was struck by the idea that she was about to embark on a journey with someone whom she barely knew. How did that happen? She smiled sheepishly when she realized Vivian had caught her staring.

"What?" asked Vivian.

"I just realized I'm trusting you, someone I just met, to know where we're going. Does that make me crazy?"

Vivian pointed over her shoulder. "That way is north." She rotated her body just a little, altering the trajectory of her pointing. "We're walking that way, northeast, for what will seem like forever."

"I'm so glad I'm not crazy."

In a matter of minutes, Vivian had instilled confidence and settled her misgivings. How did she do that? Was it the easy air of self-confidence? As if she knew exactly what she was doing? Ida might have found it annoying if Vivian weren't so damn charming about it. She somehow managed to exude confidence without all the usual trappings of ego.

"What's your last name, Vivian? I feel like I should know your full name if we're going to walk together for several days."

"Yates. And yours?"

"George." Having survived their first few minutes of one-on-one, get to know you conversation, Ida was feeling oddly encouraged about the entire adventure. *Maybe I am crazy.*

Ida wondered what Kate would say if she could see her now. Trusting her fate to a woman she was totally crushed out on and whom she'd only just met less than twenty-four hours ago. Oh yeah, she was definitely crazy.

❖

Vivian still wasn't sure why she'd agreed to escort Ida after the Franklins decided to turn back toward Natchez. There was something about Ida that stirred Vivian. Even having known Ida for only a few hours before agreeing to travel with her, the thought of Ida alone on the road unnerved her. Vivian had the unfamiliar desire to protect Ida. From what, she was unsure. For all her talk about not needing anyone and not wanting anyone to depend on her, Vivian found herself enjoying the fact that maybe Ida needed her. Being needed, even in the most superficial way, made Vivian feel a little less lonely. It didn't mean they were going to end up in a relationship or anything.

Vivian was never very good at small talk, so she wasn't very confident about making conversation. Although, to Vivian's surprise, conversation somehow came easy with Ida. Ida had a quick sense of humor, which Vivian appreciated. She quickly discovered that Ida continually caught her off guard by reacting in unexpected ways. Vivian acknowledged to herself that she'd made particular judgments about Ida based solely on her more feminine appearance. For example, she expected Ida to be spooked by a rather large pit viper slinking across the dry roadbed in front of them, but instead Ida was fascinated by the way it moved. Despite her soft, friendly demeanor, Ida seemed almost fearless.

Lunch consisted of two strips of cured beef and some corn cakes that Ida had cooked over the fire the previous night. They found a shady spot and reclined opposite each other, each leaning against her own tree.

"So, do you have family in Georgia?" Vivian asked.

"Yes, that's why I'm going there. That's where I grew up. My brother and his family are still there. And you?"

Vivian realized that the problem with asking a personal question of Ida meant that she had to answer one as well.

"No."

She realized that answer wasn't going to be satisfactory and would inevitably lead to more questions.

"Why are you going there?"

Vivian chewed the dried beef thoughtfully.

"The Blue Mountains are the ancestral home of the Cherokee Nation."

"You're Cherokee then?"

"Half Cherokee. My father was of German descent."

Vivian didn't want to get into her whole family tree, which no doubt was a bit more non-traditional than Ida's.

They ate in silence for a few more minutes before Ida asked another question.

"What do you think you'll find when you get there?"

"I'm not sure."

That wasn't entirely true. Vivian was hoping to feel some connection to her ancestors. Her grandfather talked often of the Cherokee belief that the dead walked among the trees at night. She had a strong desire to find out if he was right. But she wasn't going to say any of this to Ida.

"I think I'm making this journey in honor of my grandfather. It was his dream to travel to the Blue Mountains. He died before he could make the trip."

"I'm sorry about your grandfather."

Vivian figured that Ida was smart enough to realize there was more to the story than Vivian was sharing. She liked that Ida seemed intuitive. Ida would no doubt make a great friend, but Vivian didn't know if they could be friends. In order for that to happen, Vivian would have to overcome the growing attraction she was feeling for her. Vivian couldn't deny the fact that she had felt physically drawn to Ida the moment she'd seen her. She wondered now if the attraction was mutual.

When they finished their lunch, Ida stopped Vivian before she could lift her pack.

"Before you do that, let me see how the burn looks."

Vivian hesitated. The thought of being touched again wasn't going to lessen the attraction she was feeling for Ida. But she obliged.

Ida was several inches shorter than Vivian, and it was clear by how her clothing subtly gripped her body that she had a very pleasing feminine shape. The summer-light cotton shirt clung seductively to the swell of her breasts, and the curve of her hips filled out the barely loose fitting slacks in all the right places. Vivian stood frozen, noticing all of these details as Ida loosened the top buttons of her shirt.

They were standing so close that Vivian could smell the faint aroma of Ida's cologne, which carried a hint of lavender. The opening at the neck of Ida's blouse also gave Vivian a tantalizing view of her cleavage. Vivian closed her eyes and exhaled in an attempt to slow her ever-increasing heart rate.

"I'm sorry. Did moving the shirt disturb the wound?"

"No." Vivian tried to keep her voice even, but her mind had other ideas. Her mind imagined how Ida's lips would feel. She opened her eyes and looked down into the cool blue of Ida's. "It's not the burn that's making me uncomfortable."

"Oh." Ida seemed self-conscious and took a step back, putting space between them. She cleared her throat. "It looks less agitated than it did last night. I think the salve helped. I could make more of it tonight when we camp if you like."

"Sure, if you don't mind."

The increased physical distance between them broke the spell. Vivian sighed, smiled faintly, and buttoned her shirt again.

They walked for several more hours without much conversation. When the shadows lengthened, signaling late afternoon, they looked for a good spot to camp for the night.

Luckily, Vivian was incredibly skilled with a bow. It was a gift, that's what her grandfather had said. She could strike with an arrow through the eye of even the smallest of prey from thirty paces or more. On this evening, Vivian's first arrow had rewarded them with a rather good-sized rabbit. Similar to their first meal together, Vivian skinned and cleaned the rabbit before she settled down against a tree to watch Ida cook for them. Ida contributed a potato and some wild onions she had foraged for their evening meal.

It was clear to Vivian as she watched Ida work that cooking brought Ida joy. She seemed to take pleasure from cooking, a task that Vivian endured only out of necessity.

"Can I ask you a favor?" Ida gave Vivian a sideways glance as she stirred the food.

"You mean besides the favor where I escort you across two territory boundaries and into North Georgia?"

"Hey, I didn't ask, you offered."

"So I did," said Vivian, smiling playfully. "Okay, what's the favor?"

"Will you teach me to shoot your bow?"

"Seriously?"

"Yes, seriously." Ida took a seat on the ground nearby. "I've always wanted to learn, but my father didn't think it was appropriate for some reason."

"If you want to learn then I'll show you. It's a good skill to master, in my opinion."

"Great."

Ida returned her attention to the food. She filled two bowls and handed one to Vivian.

Traveling with Ida had offered Vivian a distraction from dwelling entirely on the awful violence she experienced at the Hudson Ranch and by the hand of Elizabeth. But part of Vivian wanted to hold on to her anger. She intended to use it to construct a wall around her heart so that she wouldn't so easily trust again. It felt like the minute she let her guard down, she inevitably ended up getting hurt. How did she always miss the signs? Were there signs to miss? Obviously, she couldn't trust her judgment either way. But as she quietly ate the food Ida had just prepared, she couldn't help but want to know more about Ida. She was mulling over what to ask when Ida spoke first.

"Have you been with lots of women?"

Vivian almost choked on her food. "What?"

"I was just thinking that women must find you very attractive."

Vivian paused with her fork midair, not sure how to respond. Ida wasn't saying that *she* thought Vivian was attractive, but that other women might.

"I think I could say the same thing about you," said Vivian.

"I'm sorry. I shouldn't have asked you such a direct question."

"I'm beginning to think you excel at direct questioning. Were you just trying to find out if I prefer women?"

"Maybe. And do you? Prefer relationships with women?"

"Yes. Most of the time."

"Most of the time?"

"Well, either relationships with women or no relationship at all. Lately, I've had some bad experiences."

"Oh, I'm sorry."

"And you?" Vivian thought she knew the answer, but now she wanted to hear Ida say it.

"I've been involved with women, although I haven't had many experiences."

Vivian couldn't believe they were talking about this so explicitly. She thought maybe putting everything out in the open might lessen the tension between them, but she found herself more stimulated than soothed by this conversation.

"You're very pretty." There, Vivian said it.

"Really?"

"Yes, really. Beautiful, in fact."

Vivian didn't know what to say after that. They quietly finished their food. Vivian was still seated when Ida bent close to retrieve her bowl so that she could clean it. Ida leaned toward Vivian, their faces so close that Vivian could feel the heat from Ida's skin. Her lips were so close, too. *Just kiss her. Just kiss her.* But Vivian vacillated and the moment passed. She looked away and gave her flustered attention over to stoking the fire.

Ida shook her head in disbelief that she'd actually asked Vivian so directly about her preferences. It was almost as if she had just blurted out the question she meant to only ponder internally. She wondered now what Vivian must be thinking of her.

The attraction she'd been feeling for Vivian didn't seem to be decreasing, but only becoming harder to ignore the more time they spent together, which so far had only been one day. She was in real trouble if this trek took more than a week, and she knew it would.

She could have sworn that Vivian was about to kiss her just now. Ida had given her the perfect opportunity, but she hadn't. *Why?* Maybe Vivian just meant she was "pretty" in the empirical sense, not in the *I think you're pretty* sense.

After she finished cleaning their dishes, Ida returned to the campfire to find Vivian had already made herself a bed. She was partially covered with the blanket and using her satchel as a pillow. Ida was a little disappointed that they weren't going to continue their conversation, but maybe that was for the best. She'd obviously made Vivian feel uncomfortable.

The night was pleasantly warm, but Ida still wanted the reassuring weight of a blanket wrapped around her shoulders. The feel of the fabric encircling her would help her sleep. Sleeping in the open air had never been a favorite pastime for Ida. As she settled in for the night, she realized this trip would likely test all her limits. Her body was fatigued, but her mind was ablaze with thoughts of Vivian. Sleep would be a while in coming.

CHAPTER TEN

Ida woke the next morning to find Vivian quietly watching her sleep. She didn't think the hour was late, but it had taken her forever to fall asleep and now she'd slept later than usual and Vivian had let her. Blinking and yawning, Ida turned on her side to face Vivian.

"Good morning." Vivian smiled.

It almost felt like a *morning after* smile, and that made Ida wonder what Vivian had been thinking while watching her sleep.

They had a couple of apples for breakfast and then began their walk. It was already warm and the sun's position suggested it was barely past nine o'clock.

The arid road seemed to stretch on forever. They walked most of the day, taking a few long breaks in the shade, although the temperature in the shade was hardly discernibly different from standing in the sun. Southern Mississippi felt like an oven prepped for baking pies.

During one of their breaks, Vivian offered to give Ida her first lesson with the bow.

"I always wanted to learn the things my brother did, but my father just didn't think I could. Or at least that's what he seemed to believe." Ida lowered her pack to the ground. "When I pressed him he could never give me a good reason why. I know now that he was probably just trying to protect me, but back then he used to make me so angry."

"It's hard for me to believe that anyone would grow up not

knowing how to hunt or defend themselves. Especially a woman, and especially these days." Vivian extracted an arrow from the quiver she usually carried over her shoulder and moved off the road with bow in hand to find them an easy target. "Once you learn to shoot accurately, do you think you'd be able to kill something?"

"I appreciate that hunting, in the abstract, is a much easier concept than the reality of taking a life. But it's my goal to be more self-sufficient, so I guess we'll find out, won't we?"

"Yeah, I suppose we will."

Ida followed Vivian off the path into an open space facing some rather large pine trees.

"Well, first things first. Your goal when hunting with a bow is all about precision."

Ida nodded to show that she was paying attention.

Vivian handed the bow to Ida. "Are you right-handed or left-handed?"

"Right-handed."

"So am I, so that'll be easier since my bow is better suited for right-handed use." Vivian stepped behind Ida so that she could help her with a proper stance. "Right-handed people are usually right-eye dominant. That means you want to hold the bow in your left hand and pull back with your right."

Vivian took the bow from Ida briefly to demonstrate, then handed it back to her. "Let's see how you hold it."

Ida labored to pull the bowstring taut. It was much harder than she expected it to be, and her arm shook from the pressure of holding the bow in the ready position.

"Before you release an arrow maybe you should roll this sleeve down. Until you're more practiced you'll want your arm covered so the bow string doesn't scrape the skin when you let go."

Vivian rolled down Ida's shirtsleeve for her since she had the bow in one hand and the arrow in the other. Vivian's fingers brushed the soft underside of Ida's arm ever so lightly as she unrolled the sleeve, which left Ida craving more contact.

Ida appreciated that Vivian was taking this lesson very seriously. She thought Vivian was absolutely adorable.

"Okay, now your body should be perpendicular to the target and the shooting line."

"What's that mean?" Ida looked down at her feet as if that would tell her if she was in the right position or not.

"It means that if you drew an imaginary line from you to the target, this line would go across the middle of your feet."

Vivian stepped close behind Ida. Vivian put her hands on Ida's hips and turned her into a better position but didn't move away from her. Instead, Vivian put her arms around Ida to help her adjust into the proper shooting stance.

"Hold the bow with your left hand, point your left shoulder to the target, and take the arrow and string with your right hand. Keep your feet about shoulder-width apart." Vivian's mouth was very close to Ida's ear when she said, "Try to relax."

As if. Had Ida not already been nervous enough to attempt to shoot, she was certainly a bundle of nerves now. Vivian was standing so close against her back that Ida could feel her warmth and smell her spicy, earthy scent. Ida closed her eyes in an attempt to calm her libido. She didn't want Vivian to know how strongly their close proximity was affecting her. *Breathe. She's just showing you how to use a bow, not asking you for a date.*

"Attach the back of the arrow to the bow string and then use three fingers to lightly hold the arrow on the string. Like this." Vivian covered Ida's hand so she could demonstrate. "Then draw the string hand toward your face to an anchor point. The anchor is usually somewhere around your chin, cheek, ear, or the corner of your mouth. Whatever you use as your anchor point, remember it so that your shots will be consistent."

Ida felt the heat of Vivian's hand over hers as she demonstrated the proper pull and anchor, but Ida now barely remembered what she was even trying to learn. All she could think about was how close Vivian's lips were to the edge of her ear and the feel of Vivian's firm body pressed against her.

"Let go," Vivian said, as she removed her hand to allow Ida to control the release of the arrow.

The minute Vivian removed her hand, Ida dropped her arm so

that the arrow shot into the dirt about ten feet away. Vivian watched with consternation on her face.

"What were you aiming at? I—"

Before the words were out of her mouth, Ida had turned into Vivian, wrapped her arms around Vivian's neck, and pulled her down into a kiss. At first, Vivian tensed. She seemed unsure of what to do with her hands. But when Ida refused to release her hold on Vivian's neck, she leaned into Ida and pulled her even closer into a deep and heated kiss.

Ida released Vivian's lips only for a moment. "I was aiming for this." She ran her fingers through Vivian's thick hair and leaned into a luxurious kiss, slowing the movement of her tongue as if savoring every slight contact between them. Her heart thundered in her chest and between her legs. As far as first kisses go, Ida declared this one epic. Earth-shattering. Soul searching. Passionate. Sweet. *God, Vivian is a great kisser.*

The bow and quiver of arrows lay on the ground next to them, forgotten. Ida felt Vivian press her hips against hers; despite the heat of late summer, they could not get close enough. After a little while, the kiss slowed, and they released each other, breathless and flushed.

"Your aim is amazingly good."

Ida laughed. "However, I think I may need another lesson with the bow."

"Only if I can get another kissing lesson."

Ida smiled and grabbed the front of Vivian's shirt, pulling her close so that she could stand on her toes and kiss her lightly on the mouth again.

"You, Vivian Yates, are an amazing kisser. I don't think you need any lessons at all, but practice never hurts."

After a few more kisses, Vivian retrieved the arrow from where it had struck the dirt. They gathered their things and began walking again. Every now and then they smiled shyly at each other as they made their way east, away from the setting sun.

Chapter Eleven

After enduring a second day of the stagnant heat and having just crossed into Alabama, the sight of Bonita Lake was glorious. They dropped their packs and walked into the cool water, clothes and all.

Vivian just happened to be looking in Ida's direction when Ida stood up in the waist-deep water where her wet blouse clung to the soft curves of her upper body. Vivian couldn't help but notice the pleasing round shape of her breasts and her firm nipples coming to hard points and pushing against the clinging fabric. Ida looked down, aware of what Vivian was looking at, and then blushed and dropped back into the water.

"I'm so embarrassed!"

"You shouldn't be. You're beautiful." Vivian swam a little closer to where Ida had submerged herself in the shallow lake. Vivian was finding it more and more difficult to fight the attraction she felt for Ida. They'd kissed a few times since that first kiss, and even though Vivian had conspired to keep her emotional distance, the physical attraction just seemed to keep building between them.

Vivian swam to within a foot of where Ida was and stood up, the water hitting her at her waist. As had been the case with Ida's shirt, Vivian's shirt also clung tightly to her chest, outlining her tight breasts.

"I'm not beautiful, but thank you," Ida said.

"Stand up." Vivian extended her hands to Ida.

Ida stood slowly, watching Vivian's face as she rose out of the water. Vivian pressed closer to her, allowing her hands to rest at Ida's waist. Ida rested her hands, cool from the water, on Vivian's forearms. Vivian looked down, noticing the contrast between Ida's fair complexion and her bronze arms.

"Maybe this is a good time for more practice." They began to kiss softly, and Vivian teased Ida's mouth with her tongue. The press of their bodies together, despite the damp clothing, was setting Vivian on fire. She began to move her hands up from Ida's slim waist to the rounded contours of her breasts. Her thumb brushed across Ida's erect nipple through the thin fabric of her damp blouse, leaving Ida shuddering, moaning softly into their kiss.

"I don't suppose you'd want to take your shirt off?" said Vivian. She sensed Ida smiling against her lips.

"Vivian Yates, are you making a pass at me?"

"Yes." Vivian began to slowly unbutton the front of Ida's shirt. "Yes, Ida George, I am most definitely making a pass at you."

"It took you long enough."

They only broke their kiss long enough to slip out of their clothes. Once they were fully nude, Vivian pulled them into deeper water. Vivian was a few inches taller, so she could stand, but Ida had to cling to Vivian since she couldn't touch bottom. Vivian teased her, pulling Ida along and moving toward her so that their bodies touched. The feel of their breasts contacting in the cool lake water gave Vivian an ache deep inside that settled into her stomach before moving further down. They kissed and explored each other. Ida arched into Vivian's hand as she caressed her breast.

Vivian began a slow survey of Ida's soft, rounded form. She traced her fingertips all along the outside curve of Ida's breasts, down across her ribs, and to her hips, before making the slow return journey to bury her fingers into Ida's hair. As she moved her hands up and down Ida's body, she felt Ida press into her.

Vivian wanted Ida. But in the short time she'd spent with Ida, she sensed that Ida was looking for more than just a physical connection. And a physical connection was all Vivian was willing to offer at the moment. She figured they should slow down or she wasn't going to be able to stop. Ida seemed to have no idea of the effect she was having on Vivian.

"Hey, should we get out of the water for a while?" Vivian asked. She kissed Ida's lips between every other word.

"Maybe we should." Ida was still pressed against the length of her body. "We should either get out of the water or stay here forever."

Vivian watched the sunset dance in Ida's eyes. Her heart felt light; she almost felt as if she could just float away. But then she reminded herself not to care. She reminded herself to keep Ida at a safe distance. Vivian closed her eyes and dropped her head under the water's surface in an attempt to cool her raging libido. Then she began to pull them toward the shore.

Ida watched Vivian as she disappeared behind some trees to change clothes. Something had shifted. Something had happened between their flirtation in the water and the swim back to shore. It was as if a stone wall had gone up between them. Ida had sensed Vivian's playful mood change to one of reserved distance as if a cool wind had just swept through their camp. The sudden shift after what felt like such intimacy scared her a little. Ida's intuition was sending her impulses to be cautious with Vivian, but the attraction she felt was hard to temper.

After they were both no longer bare, Ida helped Vivian go about the tasks of setting up camp for the night, gathering wood, and building a small fire. Vivian fashioned a long spear and waded back into the lake to capture some fish for dinner. She seemed lost in her own world, solely focused on her task.

As Ida watched from the water's edge, she realized she'd wanted to kiss Vivian since the first moment they met. She wanted to do much more than kiss Vivian. Her emotional response to Vivian's touch was strong. How could she tell Vivian that all she had to do was touch her once to send her into an emotional frenzy? She shook her head, smiling; it was probably best to keep that detail to herself.

They camped for two more days by the lake, taking frequent respites from the heat in its cooling water. They swam, coming together to kiss and embrace but careful not to move their sexual play beyond a certain point. It was as if they were both savoring just the act of getting to know each other. They were having fun. And the more time they spent together, the more relaxed they became with each other.

On the beginning of their third day, they returned to their northeastern trek.

While crossing East Mississippi into Alabama, they had only been able to kill a few squirrels and rabbits for food, punctuated late one afternoon by a patch of ripe blackberries. If it had been closer to autumn they'd have surely found pecans on the ground, but it was too early in the growing cycle.

After a tiring day of walking, they made camp and sat around the small cook fire they had made together. Ida reclined against her small pack with her legs stretched out toward Vivian. Vivian propped herself against her bag, pointing her body toward Ida. Gently, Vivian removed Ida's ankle-high boots, pulled her legs across her lap, and began to rub Ida's feet.

Ida moaned with pleasure. "That feels so good."

Vivian smiled but remained silent.

Ida thought they had become more comfortable with each other, but still Vivian didn't talk much about herself or what she was feeling. Ida wanted to know more about this woman she couldn't stop wanting to touch.

The light from the campfire flickered across Vivian's strong features, and Ida thought she saw the shadow of some dark thought pass across Vivian's face. She looked away for a moment into the low flames of the fire, not meeting Ida's gaze.

"What were you thinking just now?" asked Ida.

"Nothing."

"It didn't seem like nothing."

"I'm not very good at talking about feelings." Vivian shifted and began rubbing her thumbs across the underside of Ida's other foot.

"Everyone has a hard time talking about their feelings. Sometimes, when it's important, you just have to make yourself say the things that matter."

The sky was fully dark now, and only the glow from the campfire illuminated them. Tree frogs sang in the distance.

"'The things that matter.'" Vivian repeated the words. "Maybe what I was thinking wasn't as serious as you think."

"Just tell me what you were thinking." Ida reached out and shoved Vivian's foot playfully.

"I was thinking that I want to kiss you, everywhere."

"Everywhere?"

"Everywhere." Vivian's fingers were moving slowly around Ida's feet.

"Show me."

Vivian moved close so that she could press her mouth firmly onto Ida's. The sexual tension that had been building since their first kiss seemed to explode between them like a wildfire across dry brush. As her tongue found entrance and the kiss deepened, Vivian pushed into Ida from her kneeling position so that Ida had to lie back onto the ground. Vivian gently lay on top of her. The full press of their bodies together felt so amazingly good. Vivian began to stroke her hands up and down Ida's abdomen and the side of her breasts as Ida moaned softly beneath her. She pressed her thigh between Ida's legs and continued her advance. She felt Ida's fingers run through the hair at the back of her neck, pulling Vivian's mouth more firmly against her own. It felt like Ida wanted this as much as she did.

Ida grabbed Vivian's fingers as they fidgeted with her top's buttons and slipped her hand inside. Vivian's mouth was luscious and relentless. Ida had never been kissed with such intensity. She had to break the kiss and catch her breath. When she pulled away, she felt Vivian hesitate.

"No, Vivian, don't stop. Please don't stop. I just needed to catch my breath."

Vivian set upon Ida's neck, down to the space between her breasts, and to the smooth sensitive skin of her navel. Vivian pulled the fabric of her bra aside and took Ida's nipple into her mouth.

Ida gasped. "Oh, my God. Don't stop." She held handfuls of Vivian's thick dark hair in her fingers as Vivian lovingly kissed first one breast and then the other.

Ida felt constricted by her own clothes. "Wait, let me take this off."

Vivian pulled her mouth away just long enough for Ida to bare her breasts fully.

Ida didn't want to give Vivian any reason to stop, but she desperately wanted inside Vivian's shirt, to feel her skin. She hesitantly reached for the buttons. That was the only hint Vivian needed. She sat up and quickly got rid of her shirt, then pressed her bare chest against Ida's. The arousal was immediate. Ida felt the most excruciating ache between her legs.

Even in the low light from the dying fire Ida could see the wild darkness in Vivian's eyes. She'd seen it the first night they'd met. She felt Vivian move to touch her between her legs, but Ida stopped her, capturing Vivian's wrist with her hand. Ida spoke softly against Vivian's neck, "Wait, I don't know if I'm ready to go that far."

Vivian pulled back and looked at Ida's face. "We can wait, but I should tell you that you're driving me crazy." Vivian kissed Ida's neck and her chest again.

"I'm making myself crazy."

Vivian trailed kisses all along Ida's neck and shoulders while still pressing her leg between Ida's thighs. Ida moaned with pleasure, continuing to run her fingers through Vivian's mane. After being excruciatingly attentive to Ida's breasts, Vivian rolled off her, breathing hard. Vivian seemed so aroused that she had to pull away from Ida for a moment to calm down.

Lying beside each other on the ground, Ida sensed Vivian's mood shift. It was the same as it had been that day in the lake. She felt Vivian closing down, and it was as if a cold draft wafted across her bare chest. She shivered and reached for her shirt to cover herself. What had just happened?

Vivian sat up beside her. After a moment, she turned and gave Ida a weak smile.

"I'm going to go get a bit more wood for the fire." Vivian pulled on her shirt as she stood.

She walked away, leaving Ida shirtless and confused.

Chapter Twelve

At some point during the night, Ida was awakened by a caress on her arm. It must have been deep in the night because the stars were twinkling brilliantly against the infinite blackness.

"You're awake?"

"I'm sorry, I couldn't sleep. And I couldn't help touching you." Vivian traced Ida's arm with her fingertips and placed a kiss on Ida's forehead.

After the fire had died down, they had fallen asleep nestled in each other's arms, Ida's head tucked into the hollow space in Vivian's shoulder. The sensation of being cradled in Vivian's arms was the most wonderful thing Ida had experienced in a long time. Ida grazed Vivian's neck with her lips. Maybe she'd just imagined Vivian's emotional distance earlier. Things felt different now. She was hopeful that they had finally crossed some barrier. Their closeness felt good.

Vivian stroked Ida's hair and then her back, making circular motions. The heat of their bodies pressed together was simultaneously electric and soothing for Ida.

"What's your middle name?" Ida asked. "I feel like that's something I should know now."

"Wildfire."

"How perfect." Ida's lips curled into a smile against Vivian's shoulder. "You are a wildfire, Vivian Yates."

"The day I was born, there were huge grass fires on the plains in Oklahoma, ignited by lightning. My grandfather took it as a sign that this should be my name."

"Your name is magical. My middle name isn't nearly as exciting. It's May. Ida May George. And my mother used all three names when I did something that displeased her. 'Ida May George,' she'd yell."

After relating the story to Vivian, her mood shifted.

"Is something wrong?" Vivian asked.

"I miss my mother." Ida closed her eyes. "I cared for her the last year of her life. That was partly why I traveled to the Gulf Coast with my friend Kate. The house was just too sad after Mom's passing. I needed a change of scenery."

"Are you worried the sadness will be there when you get back?"

"Maybe a little, but I miss my brother and his family. I miss the Blue Mountains more than I could have imagined. They're like a member of the family that I've lost touch with. I need to reconnect with the place I'm from."

Ida outlined the mark on Vivian's chest with her finger. "Do you mind if I ask how this happened?"

Vivian sighed.

"You don't have to tell me if you don't want to."

"It's a burn from a branding iron."

Ida stiffened next to Vivian. She couldn't imagine how much a burn like that would hurt. She waited for Vivian to explain further.

"I was working for a few weeks on this ranch, owned by a family named Hudson. The guy that ran the place was pretty awful. I sort of got involved with his sister, Elizabeth, and then I stupidly got into a fight with him. The branding iron was within reach, and Elizabeth used it to break up the fight."

"Oh, Vivian." Ida tightened her arms around Vivian's waist.

"I should have known better. I had this bad feeling that something wasn't right, and for some reason I didn't listen to my own intuition. I should never have stayed on the ranch as long as I did."

They were quiet for a few minutes in the darkness. Vivian

pulled Ida close, and Ida rested her open palm on the center of Vivian's chest. She could feel the steady pulse of Vivian's heartbeat.

"Were you in love with her?"

"No."

The response seemed too quick and without inflection.

"It was just a physical thing." Vivian tried to be nonchalant, but Ida could tell by the sadness in her voice that Elizabeth had hurt her. Vivian had obviously cared enough to feel wounded, and not just from the burn.

Vivian settled against Ida and they lay quietly together watching the stars overhead before they drifted off to sleep.

CHAPTER THIRTEEN

They woke at first light to break camp. As they went about the task of beginning their day together, Vivian realized she was grateful that Ida had gotten her to open up a little about Elizabeth. Her mood was somewhat lighter because of their discussion. She knew she still hurt from what had happened between them, but she'd been determined to bury it deep inside. Ida didn't press her to speak of it further, and Vivian didn't offer it up for examination. She wasn't quite ready to let it go entirely. In some ways, she needed the anger to remind her not to care too much. If you didn't care, no one could hurt you.

It would take them a little more than a week to get from Meridian to Oxford on the shores of Logan Martin Lake, longer if they lingered. The days were bright and the evenings were magical. Time spent with Ida was making it difficult for Vivian to keep distance between them. Sometimes she even lost sight of her anger and began to relax. Making camp every night meant time to cuddle with Ida. They would kiss, sometimes so luxuriously that Vivian had a hard time not taking things further. But Ida had asked to wait, and she was making her best effort to respect Ida's wishes. It was good that they were getting to know each other as they walked, their companionship becoming easier and more relaxed with each passing day. Sometimes when they stopped their trek for a kiss, the air around them almost seemed to crackle with an electric charge. Becoming more intimate had lessened the tension between them in some ways, but generated more in other ways.

After walking for several hours, they crested a small rise in the roadway and followed the gradual slope downward into a large valley that had once housed a wind farm. The towering remains of faded white turbines stretched as far as they could see. The spawn of nearby forest groves had reseeded the grassy valley in recent decades so that hardwoods now mixed with the sleeping metal giants.

Vivian approached the base of one of the mammoth machines and ran her palm across its cool, smooth surface. Whatever this material was, it hadn't been aged by the elements in the same manner as the ragged auto frames she'd come across earlier in her trek. But in the end, without oil, wind turbines suffered the same fate as every other mechanized system. They stalled and then stopped moving altogether. Unfortunately, people realized too late just how much oil was needed to support their last-ditch efforts to save the power substructure. There were the machines that manufactured the replacement parts for the turbine engines, and there were the heavy machines required to install and maintain the industrialized windmills, just to name a few.

Vivian could see that some of the spray-painted protest messages from long ago were still visible. A vocal few had seen the end of fossil fuels coming and had argued for their leadership to establish alternative energy sources before the oil-supported infrastructure collapsed entirely. "Oil = Death" was still legible just above where she was standing.

"Do you ever try to imagine what it must have been like in the old days?" asked Ida.

Vivian turned to face Ida, her palm still resting on the semi-worn alloy surface. "Sometimes."

"I can't really picture it even though I've seen photos in books. It doesn't seem real. It seems like something from another world."

Vivian tried to visualize the huge blades spinning, but she couldn't. Any trace of a power grid was a distant memory by the time Vivian's grandfather was a child. She'd heard the stories and read the history in books. Vivian was fascinated by how societies reacted to scarcity. It seemed to her that more often than not they divided the populace into classes, and then divided the resources accordingly with the super rich taking the biggest piece of the pie. That's what happened during the final resource grab over a century ago, when the first cloud cities began to rise. They were small at first, not much bigger than a luxury hovercraft. But as technology catered more and more to the lifestyles of the wealthy, the floating cities expanded to suspend entirely above the scarcity on the ground. Over time, life below the clouds stabilized. But the elite class stayed in the clouds. Good riddance, thought Vivian.

"My grandfather used to say the air is precious to us. The air shares its spirit with the life it supports."

"What does that mean?"

"I'm not sure." Vivian shoved her hands into her trouser pockets. "Maybe it means the air isn't meant to be captured. Or maybe it's just an admonishment to value and respect the forces of the natural world." Vivian smiled in Ida's direction. "I wish I'd asked my grandfather to explain some of his teachings in more detail. I suppose I thought there would always be plenty of time to ask more questions."

Ida stepped close to Vivian. She gently tugged Vivian's arm as she leaned close to plant a kiss on her cheek. "I'm sorry I didn't get to meet him."

❖

When they stopped later that day for a brief rest, Vivian pulled out her grandfather's tattered map. She knelt to unfold the weathered document and spread it on the ground. Ida stood behind her, looking over her shoulder. This was the first time Ida had seen the map with the hand-drawn notations.

"Can you read that?" asked Ida. "I don't recognize the language."

"Yeah, it's written in Cherokee."

"What does it say?"

"It's mostly made up of notes estimating distances, along with some descriptions of landmarks." Vivian sat back on her heels. "This map belonged to my grandfather. He would ask travelers about features of this region and then make notations on the map. I think it took him years to compile all this detail." Vivian removed her hat and ran her fingers through her sweaty hair. She began fanning herself with the brim, moving it from side to side as she studied the map. "Of course, it's all based on rumor and conjecture. My granddad never made it this far. But so far it's been pretty accurate."

"What does that inscription say?" Ida pointed to several words written in the margin.

"Wakan Tankan Nici Un." Vivian read the Cherokee words aloud. "Roughly translated, it means *May the Great Spirit walk with you.*"

"That's beautiful."

Vivian smiled up at Ida before stowing the map back inside her pack.

❖

The flat, sandy terrain of Mississippi had transitioned into low, rolling hills covered with lush greenery and speckled with small freshwater ponds as they traversed Alabama heading east. At one point while hunting, Vivian could have taken down a deer with her bow, but decided against it because she didn't want to waste what they would be unable to eat on the spot or carry with them. She kept to small game, and they offset that whenever possible with berries and the occasional peach tree. A couple of times they passed abandoned farms and were able to gather squash and tomatoes. Once, they even found a healthy stand of summer corn, which they roasted and ate with enthusiasm.

During their two-week expedition, they passed the rare traveler. Usually folks were taking livestock across the territory for barter, or they were headed to visit relatives. Custom was to pass a kind word between migrants and glean from each other bits of news about road conditions, locations for fresh water, and weather.

They were within a day's walk of the lake near the Georgia boundary and had been walking for a few hours when Ida needed to stop.

"I need to take a break." Ida lowered her pack to the roadside.

"What?"

"I have to pee."

"Oh, sorry." Vivian shifted her pack on her shoulders to allow the slight breeze to brush across her damp shirt underneath. "I'll wait here."

Vivian watched Ida disappear into the woods. Today she'd worn a summer dress, and it swayed as she moved gingerly through the brush. Vivian was studying an opening in the canopy to gauge the time of day when she heard Ida scream. She dropped her pack and took off in the direction she'd last seen her walk. Vivian's heart was pounding and tree limbs snapped at her clothing as if to deter her as she rushed toward Ida's cries.

"Over here!"

"What happened? Oh!" Vivian could see that Ida had stepped into a steel animal trap, forgotten and covered in overgrowth.

Tears were streaming down Ida's soft features. "Don't leave me, Vivian." She grabbed Vivian's forearm.

Vivian looked at her with surprise. "I'm not going to leave you."

"Please! Don't leave me!"

She took Ida by the shoulders and looked her directly in the face. "Ida, look at me. I will not leave you. Okay?" Vivian was unsure why Ida was so afraid to be abandoned. Had her guarded emotional distance been that obvious? Even still, how could she think that Vivian would leave her injured in the woods?

"I'm sorry. I didn't mean to doubt you. I...I just panicked."

"It's okay." Vivian brushed a tear from Ida's cheek gently with her thumb. "We need to get you out of this trap." Vivian studied the contraption for a moment. "When I pull this open, you need to get your foot out of there. We don't want the trap to close on it again and do more damage."

Ida nodded.

"Okay, ready?"

"Yes."

Vivian carefully began to force the two half moons of the

ancient steel trap to open. The hinges squeaked in complaint as she pulled them apart enough for Ida to remove her leg. As soon as she was clear, Vivian released her grip to allow the trap to snap shut again. Ida cried as she held her leg. The teeth of the trap had sunk into the upper part of her laced boot, and as she'd fallen, she'd wrenched her ankle.

"Oh, God, it hurts. Do you think it's broken?" Ida asked through gritted teeth.

Vivian loosened the laces and tenderly moved her fingers around the injury inside the leather, just above her ankle, which was already beginning to swell. She didn't feel any sharp edges that would have signaled a broken bone.

"I don't think it's broken. Why don't you see if you can stand?" Vivian took Ida's hands and helped her to her feet.

Ida attempted to put weight on her foot but cried out, falling against Vivian.

"Here, sit back down." Vivian lowered Ida back to a seated position. "It could be fractured and I wouldn't feel the break, but it would hurt just the same. In any event, you can't walk on it. Let me go get something we can wrap around it to maybe slow the swelling."

"You'll come right back?" Ida pleaded.

"I promise. I won't leave you. I'm just going to get my pack." She looked at Ida's terror-stricken eyes. Vivian had no idea what had driven such fear into Ida, but she wasn't going to ask her about it now. She needed to keep Ida calm and to see to her injury. After a quick reflection of her game plan, Vivian decided to take Ida to the pack instead of the other way around.

Kneeling beside Ida, she put one arm under her knees and the other behind her back. "Put your arms around my neck. I'll carry you back out to the road."

"You can't carry me. I'm too heavy."

"Please. You're about as light as a bird. Now stop arguing with me." Vivian smiled. "I know you've been wanting me to sweep you off your feet since we met. Now's your chance."

Chapter Fourteen

Vivian lifted Ida and made her way back to the road where she'd left their gear. She rummaged around in Ida's bag for a skirt, which Ida had directed her to tear at the hem for a bandage. They wrapped the leg as best they could with limited supplies. Vivian shouldered her bag, strapped Ida's bag across her chest, and bent to lift Ida again into her arms.

"You can't carry all our stuff and me."

"I'm going to have to, oh ye of little faith," said Vivian. She was trying to lighten the mood. The situation was serious, and she knew she needed to get some help for Ida or things with her leg might worsen. "I saw smoke near a cutoff about a mile back. I'm sure there's a cabin or farm or something there. We need to find you a doctor, or at the very least, a place to rest." She looked at Ida with seriousness. "You aren't going to be able to walk on that leg for a little while."

Ida didn't speak as the gravity of her situation seemed to sink in. She just nodded and put her arms around Vivian's neck as she walked them back the way they'd just traveled.

In truth, Vivian wasn't sure how far she could carry Ida, but she was going to try her best to get them to shelter. She hoped her hunch was right about the farmhouse and that the smoke she'd seen had been from a chimney and not a campfire.

After heading back down the road to where Vivian had seen the cutoff, they turned and made it another half mile when Vivian stopped and dropped on one knee. Her breathing was labored and her arms were shaking with fatigue.

"You've got to stop, Vivian. You can't keep carrying me. Rest."

"I just need a minute. Then we'll keep going." She could see that Ida's leg was beginning to show a purple bruise just above where'd they'd wrapped it, and it was definitely swelling inside the unlaced ankle-high boot.

"Let me try and walk for a while. I can hop on one foot if you help me."

Maybe Ida was right. Vivian could support most of her weight without having to support all of it, at least for a little while. They had to be getting close. The smoke Vivian had seen couldn't be that much farther away.

With one arm across Vivian's shoulder and Vivian's arm around her waist, Ida limped until she stumbled with pain from bumping her injured foot on the ground. She'd tried to keep it suspended, but they had stumbled and her foot had struck the dirt road.

"Come on, I've rested. Let me carry you a while longer," said Vivian.

Ida reluctantly agreed as Vivian lifted her again in her arms. They had only walked for maybe another ten minutes when they rounded a bend and spotted an opening in the middle of which sat a wood-sided farmhouse. The area surrounding the house contained high grass with a split-rail fence as its boundary. Vivian headed through the open gate that hung a bit askew and up the front steps of the simple, whitewashed dwelling. The porch was a tad raised, with a few steps leading up under a long overhang that extended the length of the front of the house. Several chairs and one rocker were scattered about on the porch as if waiting for company.

Vivian leaned forward so that Ida could knock on the door. They waited, but heard no sounds. Ida knocked again. This time they heard footsteps and the door slowly opened to reveal a woman, who peered suspiciously around the edge of the door.

"Hi, we don't mean to scare you, but my friend here is hurt and we need some help," said Vivian. She was breathing hard from the exertion of carrying Ida for nearly two miles.

The woman opened the door a bit wider and gave them a good once-over. She seemed to be weighing the truth of what Vivian was saying. After a moment, she nodded and stepped aside, motioning for them to enter the dark interior. The curtains were drawn, no doubt to keep the sun's heat from baking the house's interior space. It took a moment for Vivian's eyes to adjust enough to see that the woman was directing them to a room off the main living space.

"In here. There's a bed in this room." She indicated to Vivian that she should follow.

Vivian gently laid Ida on the bed and dropped the two bags she'd been carrying on the floor nearby. A wave of exhaustion and relief washed over her.

Now that her eyes had adjusted to the dim interior, she allowed herself a moment to study the woman who'd invited them in. She watched as the woman began to explore the bandage around Ida's leg. She looked to be in her mid to late thirties. She seemed thin and maybe a little tired. She was wearing cotton trousers and a plaid work shirt. Even though Vivian didn't know this woman, she somehow knew this wasn't the stranger's normal attire. The clothing seemed oversized, as if it had been borrowed from an older brother. Her light brown hair was pulled back and clasped at the back of her neck. After a moment, the woman noticed Vivian studying her, and turned to face her.

"How long ago did this happen? And can I ask, what exactly happened?" She gave Vivian a searching look as Ida slumped back on the pillows, her jaw clenched in pain.

"We were walking on the main road and stopped to take a break. She stepped in an old trap off in some brush," said Vivian. "I had seen smoke from your chimney earlier when we passed the cutoff so we doubled back, hoping to find some help."

Vivian felt fatigue wash over her, and she swayed on her feet. The woman steadied her and, placing a hand on each arm, eased Vivian backward into a nearby chair. "I think you should sit down. I'll get you some water."

She disappeared and came back with two full glass jars. "Drink this." She handed one to Vivian and then held Ida's head up so that she could drink from the other.

"My name is Rebecca."

"I'm Vivian and this is Ida."

"Thank you so much." Ida sank back into the pillows.

"The first thing we should do is get her foot elevated." Rebecca's voice carried some authority, as if she'd handled this sort of situation before.

As Vivian sat nearby, Rebecca filled a basin near the bed with water and slowly removed the cloth wrapping on Ida's leg to more closely inspect the injury. Vivian watched over her shoulder. It seemed as if the leather upper of the boot had kept the jaws of the trap from puncturing the skin, but the force of the snapping closure and the subsequent fall had obviously done more than a little damage to Ida's ankle. The pale skin around and above her ankle was distended and purplish. Rebecca took clean strips of cloth and wrapped Ida's leg again, propping it up a little on a pillow after she'd finished.

"I have something that will help with the pain. I'll be just a minute."

Rebecca left them alone in the room. Ida reached out for Vivian's hand, which she accepted. Vivian allowed their fingers to entwine. "Everything is going to be okay," Vivian said.

Rebecca returned with a small cup in her hand. She sat on the edge of the bed and helped Ida drink. "This is a willow and meadowsweet compound. It will help dull the pain." She placed a gentle hand on Ida's forehead. "You rest. I'll bring you some food in a little while."

"Thank you so much for your kindness," said Ida.

Before Vivian followed Rebecca out of the room, she leaned over to caress Ida's hair. "Are you okay?"

"Thanks to you. I still can't believe you carried me so far."

"My arms can." Vivian was seated on the edge of the bed, smiling, still holding Ida's hand.

"I promise to give you a rubdown when I'm able."

"Hmm, I'll hold you to that promise." Vivian leaned down and kissed Ida, savoring the feel of Ida's soft lips. "I'll go talk to Rebecca and maybe get us some food. You rest and I'll be right back."

"Thank you, Vivian, for everything."

"Ida, I want you to know you can count on me. I won't let you down."

Vivian wasn't sure why she'd said those words, but for some reason she needed to, even if just to hear them for herself. She would do her best to live up to them. Even if she was attempting to guard her heart, she wasn't the sort of person who would abandon someone in need. Ever. She wanted Ida to know that. Vivian released Ida's hand as she turned to leave the room, but before she stepped through the door, she turned to say one more thing. "I'll be right outside that door if you need me, okay?"

Ida nodded, smiling weakly up at Vivian from her reclined position.

Vivian didn't really want to leave Ida alone in her fragile condition, but she needed to discuss some sort of shelter arrangement with the woman who'd taken them in. Maybe they could figure out a way to stay for a few days to allow Ida's leg to heal.

It was late afternoon, close to the dinner hour Vivian guessed. Rebecca was in the kitchen, busy at a large cast iron wood stove.

"Why don't you sit down? You must be exhausted." Rebecca motioned for Vivian to sit at the kitchen table. "I was just about to start something for dinner when I heard your knock."

Vivian dropped into one of the straight-backed chairs that surrounded the rectangular, heavy wooden table. She realized she was exhausted. After walking almost a full day, then carrying Ida for two miles, she was spent. She looked down at herself and became conscious of the fact that her clothing was covered with dirt. *No wonder Rebecca had second thoughts about letting us in. I'm a mess.*

"After I put these vegetables on to cook I can find you some clean clothes." It was as if Rebecca had read her mind. "I might have something that would fit you."

"Thanks. I just realized how awful I look."

"You two had been walking for a while?" Rebecca partially turned in Vivian's direction as she cut up potatoes and carrots and dropped them into a pot on the stovetop. Rebecca stopped for a moment, opened the stove door, and stoked the wood fire before continuing with the food prep.

"Yes, we'd been walking for a while."

"So, you two are, um, you're together then?"

Vivian froze. Were they together? Not really. They hadn't discussed anything, but saying they were a couple seemed safer than saying they weren't. Plus, if Rebecca thought they were together then she could avoid any potentially awkward moments that might develop.

"Yes, we are."

As soon as Vivian made the statement, she wondered if it were true. They were becoming friends, but they were already something else as well. Did that mean they were on their way to becoming a couple? She realized they hadn't yet given it a name. Was she ready for the responsibility of what being a couple meant? She'd just promised Ida that she wouldn't let her down. Why had she said that? It was as if her head wanted to preserve her autonomy, but her heart was drawn to Ida in a way that was hard to control. She'd definitely been letting things progress with Ida as they'd traveled together. Even though they hadn't made love she was sure Ida was probably thinking of them as a couple. Her resolve for keeping emotional distance between them was weakening and she knew it.

There was silence for a little while except for the sound of Rebecca's knife on the cutting board. The house seemed tidy, but there was an atmosphere about it, almost as if sadness occupied a space in the room like an old worn sofa. The room seemed to carry an invisible weight. And Vivian was still puzzled about the way Rebecca was dressed.

After Rebecca finished her preparation for what looked like a vegetarian stew, she joined Vivian at the table. They studied each other for a moment. Neither of them seemed unnerved by the direct gaze of the other. Vivian decided to speak first.

"Do you live here alone?"

"I do now. I had a husband." Rebecca rubbed her fingers

together, studying where a callus was beginning to form. "He died a little over eight months ago of pneumonia."

"I'm sorry to hear that."

"Yes, it's been a bit hard to keep things up."

They sat in silence. Rebecca studying some mark on the table, but not seeming to really focus on it, Vivian studying Rebecca.

"I don't mean to impose, but maybe if we could rest here for a few days I could be of some help to you." She let that suggestion sink in before continuing. "I've had experience working on farms. There's not much I can't do."

Rebecca studied Vivian's face before she responded, as if looking for some hint of dishonesty or malice.

"Okay, maybe we can help each other out for a few days." Rebecca extended an open palm across the table, which Vivian accepted. "I could use the help."

"Thank you for trusting me," said Vivian.

"You're welcome." The corners of Rebecca's mouth turned up into an easy smile. "Now, let me see about getting you some fresh clothes."

CHAPTER FIFTEEN

Ida lay quietly in the spare bedroom listening to the muffled voices from the kitchen. She knew Rebecca and Vivian were talking, but she couldn't make out the details of what they were saying. The light in the bedroom was growing dim as the sun sank. Even though her leg ached, she was enjoying the soft bed. She was aware that her clothes were worn and dirty and that she was wearing the miles they'd traveled. Maybe she'd be able to take a bath and change tomorrow, when hopefully her leg wouldn't hurt quite as much.

Reflecting on what had just happened, Ida couldn't quite figure out why she'd panicked about being left by Vivian. Was there something about Vivian that led her to believe she would abandon someone when they were injured? Was she just afraid that Vivian would leave her eventually? Vivian did give the impression of restless searching. Searching for what, Ida wasn't sure. She half expected Vivian to bolt the moment they got their first view of the Blue Mountains. And despite the days they'd spent alone together, Ida still had not quite been able to bridge the final distance with her. A space existed between them that she had been unable to traverse. If Vivian was having any second thoughts about their involvement, this would certainly be the perfect excuse to part company and keep traveling on her own. But Vivian hadn't left her. Vivian had been a solid, calming presence, soothing Ida's fears without condescension or ridicule.

Ida wondered what they were talking about in the kitchen. Even though she hadn't known Vivian for long, she knew her well enough to know that small talk was not one of her strengths. Ida smiled at the thought of Vivian struggling to make friendly conversation with a complete stranger.

❖

Vivian had excused herself to bathe and change while Rebecca finished dinner. She returned to the kitchen wearing the borrowed clothing that Rebecca had provided and felt refreshed. Rebecca turned from the pot she was stirring and gasped. Vivian glanced down. It dawned on her that she was probably wearing Rebecca's husband's shirt and trousers. She felt sorry for any sadness she'd just brought fresh to the surface.

"Sorry, I didn't mean to shock you," said Vivian. "The fit is pretty good."

"No." Rebecca cleared her throat. "No, you didn't shock me, it's just—" She stopped what she was doing and gave Vivian her full attention. "You're about the same height as Eric was. And seeing you in his clothes, well, it just gave me a small jolt."

"I'm very sorry for your loss. And I thank you for your charity. The clothes and the food are greatly appreciated." Vivian shoved her hands in her front pockets, not really knowing what else to say. "I'll begin making it up to you tomorrow. Just tell me what needs doing."

Rebecca smiled. "This stew is about done. Would you like to take a bowl in to Ida? I doubt she'd feel like sitting at the table. Then you and I can eat out here if you like." Rebecca served up a heaping bowl of the stew and handed it to Vivian.

Vivian knocked lightly at the door that had been left slightly open for Ida's sake. "Ida, are you awake?"

"Yes, I'm awake. Maybe you could light the lantern by the bed."

Vivian handed Ida the bowl of food and lit the lantern on the small bedside table near Ida. The soft golden glow grew and warmed the room.

"This smells good. I'm starving." She couldn't seem to help sampling the stew.

"We can stay here for a few days until you feel better. I worked it out with Rebecca."

"That's great."

"She needs help around the place and you need a roof over your head. And from the looks of things, she could really use some assistance."

Ida put her spoon down and her expression grew serious. "Vivian, thank you for today. I was scared. I'm sorry I freaked out on you."

"Yeah, what was that about?"

"I'm not sure." Ida looked down at the bowl of food in her lap. "I guess I was afraid you wouldn't want someone slowing you down."

"Ida, there's no way I would leave you...you know, unless you wanted me to."

"Hey, come here." Ida reached for Vivian. She pulled Vivian's lips to hers, but before she kissed Vivian she said, "I don't see that happening anytime soon."

Their lips were almost touching as they spoke in hushed tones. "How is your leg? Does it hurt much?"

"Only when I breathe."

Ida brushed her lips across Vivian's. Vivian sat on the edge of the bed so she could partially embrace Ida as they kissed.

"You smell good." Ida snuggled her nose into Vivian's freshly washed hair. "Maybe you could work out a bath and fresh clothes for me, too?"

"I'll see what I can do. I'll come back and check on you in a little while." Vivian kissed Ida one more time then walked back to the kitchen where Rebecca had set two bowls for them.

❖

Ida watched Vivian walk toward the kitchen. Vivian's long stride was easy and confident, and the borrowed shirt and trousers clung to her lean frame in just the right places. Ida felt a surge of arousal just by noticing these details and turned away to finish the stew that Vivian had delivered. She hadn't expected to fall for anyone, nor had she wanted to, but now that someone had captured her attention so fully, Ida realized how lonely she'd been. Ever since Kate and John had gotten together, she'd been more on her own.

Setting the empty bowl on the side table, Ida could hear the muffled voices from the other room rise. She was sorry to miss out on the conversation between Rebecca and Vivian, but at the same time she was grateful to have some time to herself to reflect on the past few days. She wondered if Vivian would sleep in the room with her. They hadn't discussed it, and maybe under the circumstances they shouldn't. It was getting harder for Ida to pace the physical part of their budding relationship. She also knew her leg would be plenty painful, and she wanted Vivian to get some rest. She also definitely wanted to clean up before she let Vivian get close to her again. *I must look awful. And I probably smell worse than I look.*

Ida shifted and made an attempt to elevate her leg by propping it up on the footboard. That seemed to relieve some of the pressure she was feeling on her foot. She could tell even in the low light from the lantern that her leg was swollen.

In the kitchen, Vivian ate slowly while Rebecca talked about how hard it had been to keep up the small farm without Eric's help. It had been a constant struggle for the past eight months, which showed in the lines on Rebecca's face. There was always some task that needed her attention, and every day the list of tasks grew. The horse needed to be tended and fed, the eggs needed to be gathered, and there were boards at the back of the pen that needed to be replaced so there would be eggs to gather. The vegetable garden needed daily care, and then there was the canning for the winter months. Rebecca had to let small tasks go, like keeping the lawn in front of the house trimmed. The front gate was hanging off its hinges. She stopped listing her flurry of to-dos and admitted to Vivian that the whole place was in disrepair. Vivian finally also found the answer to her question about the way Rebecca was dressed. She'd been wearing

Eric's clothes of late to save what few dresses she had. She'd lost weight from all the labor, and apologized for what little attention she'd been paying to her hair.

Vivian sat silently and listened. It seemed obvious to her that Rebecca was very lonely and probably hadn't talked with anyone in quite some time. She learned that Rebecca and Eric had homesteaded the place for about six years before he became ill. She had no family nearby, and nowhere else to go.

"Sometimes, late in the night, the darkness presses in on me. From time to time I've slept with an old family Bible on my chest. Not because the words are comforting, but because the weight of it makes me feel less alone." Rebecca looked up at Vivian for the first time in several minutes. The shadows under her eyes now seemed more obvious. "I'm sorry, I've only just met you and I've sat here and talked nonstop, telling you my whole, sad life story."

"I don't mind. I'm very sorry you've had such a tough time of it."

"Everyone has tough times."

"Maybe you're due for a break."

"Maybe."

"Rebecca, I'll help in whatever way I can while Ida mends."

Rebecca smiled for the first time since she began to relay the details about her life. "It's nice to have people in the house."

"Thank you for sharing your food with us. This stew is very good. You're a good cook."

"Thank you. To be honest, it's nice to have some company for supper."

"Maybe tomorrow I could get a rabbit or a turkey for us?" Vivian leaned back in her chair.

"If you could, that'd be great. I haven't had much meat lately. I'm not very good with a bow, and I can't spare the chickens for cooking. I need the eggs more."

They ate in silence for a few minutes.

"I don't think Ida's leg is fractured, but she should stay off it for a few days just to be safe," said Rebecca.

Vivian nodded. "I was thinking I could craft a set of crutches for her tomorrow, if you have something we could pad the cross pieces with for under her arms. Then at least she could get around a little, you know, to the outhouse or kitchen."

"I think that's a good idea." Rebecca paused for a moment. "I can put a chamber pot nearby for tonight. Also, I only have the two bedrooms, so I can bring you some blankets to sleep out here in the main room if that's all right."

"That will be fine, thanks. After so many nights sleeping in the open I'll be happy for the roof and a smooth floor."

Vivian knew it would be hard to sleep knowing Ida was alone in the next room. But she figured Ida needed to rest, and Vivian wasn't sure she could keep from touching Ida if she were lying next to her. Maybe they were a couple after all. If not, they were getting close to something that felt like coupling.

Having settled on a plan, after cleaning up the supper dishes Rebecca brought blankets and a pillow for Vivian and excused herself for the night. She sensed Rebecca watching her from her bedroom door, but didn't look in that direction. Instead, Vivian set about creating a nest of blankets for herself on the plank floor near the fireplace. It had long since held a fire as the summer nights in Alabama were quite warm, but the lingering smell of wood smoke wafted from its soot-blackened interior. The scent comforted Vivian. The smell conjured childhood memories of nights spent around a stone fireplace with her grandfather.

Vivian checked on Ida. Since it was getting late, she was reluctant to disturb Rebecca too much with getting a bath for Ida, and as she peeked into the room she could see that Ida was already fast asleep.

Vivian moved back to settle into her nest of blankets. Exhaustion claimed her quickly as the soothing night murmurs of a cicada and tree frog chorus drifted to her from the open window.

CHAPTER SIXTEEN

Vivian heard sounds behind her as she sat up and rubbed her eyes with the palms of her hands. When she turned she saw Rebecca boiling coffee and making eggs. Vivian moved to join her. The smell of coffee was heavenly.

"I hope I didn't wake you."

"The sun took care of that." Vivian stretched and got to her feet. "We haven't had coffee in a while. It smells so good."

"I've been rationing the coffee, but I felt like we all deserved a cup today. There's a traveling merchant who passes by now and then who will barter with me for coffee and other goods," said Rebecca. "Unfortunately, I haven't seen him in a while. He and his son make the route between here and Meridian every few weeks or so."

"Too bad we didn't pass him along the way. I would have traded something for the small comfort of coffee."

"Vivian? Hello out there!"

Vivian and Rebecca turned as they heard Ida call from the other room. Vivian stuck her head in the door. "Good morning."

"Good morning. Outhouse! Please, and hurry!"

"At your service!" Vivian hoisted Ida and carried her out to the privy near the back of the house.

While Vivian waited she spoke to Ida through the door. "I'm going to make you some crutches today so you won't be so stranded in the house."

"Thank you," came the muffled reply.

"Did the chamber pot work last night for you?"

"Sort of. I'd rather have privacy for these sorts of necessities," said Ida with frustration in her voice. "I don't want people having to clean up after me in that way. It's completely demoralizing."

"I understand."

"I can tell you're laughing. It's not funny."

"I'm sorry. You're right, of course."

After a few moments, Ida steadied herself on the door frame enough so that Vivian could again lift her and carry her back inside. Instead of returning her to the bedroom, she settled her into a chair near the big table where Rebecca served her coffee and eggs.

"A girl could get used to this sort of treatment," said Ida.

Blond tendrils of Ida's hair, tousled from sleep, charmingly framed her face. The thought of waking up with Ida on a regular basis flashed through Vivian's mind. The fact that she liked the idea of more time with Ida spooked her a little. She cleared her throat and settled into a chair across from Ida.

"Let's have a look at that leg." Rebecca moved around the table to sit next to Ida.

"No, no, eat first. The leg will keep," said Ida. "And, Rebecca, I need to tell you that you saved my life yesterday. The food and the rest were just what I needed. Thank you."

"You're welcome."

They ate and savored the coffee before Rebecca examined Ida's injury. She pulled a chair up near Ida and propped her leg so that the injured area rested on her thigh. It was obvious that the leg was swollen, even with the bandage, which she slowly removed to have a closer look.

Rebecca wanted to put a fresh dressing on Ida's ankle, but it was decided that Ida should probably just have a good soak in the tub first and then keep the foot elevated for another day before trying to move around too much. In the meantime, while Rebecca helped Ida into a hot bath, Vivian searched about for some young saplings she could harvest and craft into crutches.

After that task was finished, Vivian returned to deliver the crutches to Ida. She knocked lightly at the bathroom door, and Ida beckoned her to enter. As soon as she stepped into the cozy room, which featured a large claw-foot tub as its centerpiece, she felt flustered. She didn't know what she'd expected to find. She knew Ida was taking a bath, but somehow it hadn't dawned on her that Ida would be nude. Vivian averted her eyes as she put the crutches on the floor within Ida's reach.

"Thank you."

Vivian heard the water splash as Ida adjusted herself to look over the side of the high-walled tub at the crutches on the floor.

"You're welcome." Vivian cleared her throat. She felt sure she was blushing and she hoped Ida hadn't noticed.

"Are you blushing?"

"Um, maybe."

"Adorable." Vivian heard the water splash again as Ida reached for her. "Come here."

Vivian sheepishly settled onto a small stool near the tub. Ida pulled her into a kiss.

"You've seen me with my clothes off before." Ida smiled teasingly at Vivian.

"I know. I don't know why I'm blushing. I just—" Ida interrupted her with another kiss. This one lasted for a few moments, making Vivian want to peel off her clothes and climb into the tub of soapy warm water with her.

"The blush looks good on you."

Vivian smiled. Ida somehow always managed to make her heart feel feather light. "Well, I should let you enjoy your bath. And I should go earn our keep."

"Vivian, thank you again for everything you're doing."

Vivian leaned close to kiss Ida again. "Stop thanking me. I want to do this, okay?"

"Okay."

"I'll see you later." Vivian smiled back at Ida, submerged in the sudsy water, as she pulled the door closed behind her.

Once outside, Vivian walked around the small farm mentally cataloging items that needed repair or attention. It was past noon before Rebecca found her, mending the loose fence rails of the horse pen. She hadn't been back to the house since she'd delivered the crutches for Ida and it was past the lunch hour. Rebecca brought a generous portion of cornbread and a glass jar of water to Vivian.

"You read my mind. I was just thinking I was hungry."

"I made the cornbread a half hour ago. It's still warm."

"Thank you," said Vivian. As she reached for the offering, Rebecca must have noticed that she had blood on the knuckles of her hand. She set the food, wrapped in a cloth napkin, on the ground beside them and captured Vivian's hand in hers.

"Let me see that. What happened?"

"Oh, nothing. Just a scrape. I wasn't paying attention using the wood planer."

Rebecca raised Vivian's injured knuckles to her lips and tenderly kissed the site of hurt. Then realizing what she'd done, released Vivian's hand as if she'd been stung by it. "Oh, I'm sorry. I'm not sure why I did that. Habit, I guess."

"Hey, it's okay." Vivian reached for Rebecca's wrist. "Rebecca, it's okay. It does feel better." Rebecca finally looked up to meet her gaze.

"Now you're just making fun of me."

"No really, it hardly hurts at all now," said Vivian playfully. She reached for the cornbread and made quick work of it, along with the cool liquid. "Thank you for this."

"Don't forget to drink plenty. It's hot today." Rebecca spoke over her shoulder as she turned and made her way back to the house.

Vivian watched her retreating figure, once again clad in Eric's oversized clothing, cinched with a wide leather belt at her waist, before returning to her task. Such a caring and attentive woman shouldn't be alone. Vivian hoped that love would find Rebecca again.

CHAPTER SEVENTEEN

Over the next several days, they settled into a domestic sorority. Ida's leg was sore, but mending well enough. Although still dependent on the crutches, she was feeling up to assisting the others with cooking and small tasks around the house such as laundry and cleaning.

Rebecca settled into a rhythm with Vivian. She helped her with certain farm tasks that required more than one pair of hands. Vivian seemed better suited to the heavier labor that Eric used to shoulder. Rebecca was even back to wearing her own clothes. Rebecca kept pointing out to the others that the dresses were nothing fancy, but on more than one occasion, Ida had commented on how the soft floral cotton patterns set off her light brown hair nicely. She also seemed lighter in both mood and movement when wearing them. As if she was feeling more comfortable in her own skin.

Ida was enjoying the time at Rebecca's farm. After traveling and camping for all those days, she realized she definitely wasn't a wanderer at heart. She preferred hearth and home to the freedom of the wild. But this wasn't home, and as much as she enjoyed Rebecca's hospitality, she was anxious to see her brother and his family. She was also equally anxious for things to move forward with Vivian. Being in someone else's home, and contending with her injury, had required a separation that was starting to make Ida more than a little impatient. She wanted time alone with Vivian. She wanted Vivian to sleep with her in the same room, in the same bed.

On the fourth night of their stay at Rebecca's, Ida was in bed mulling over all these things in her head when the door opened slowly and revealed Vivian. Almost as if she'd called to Vivian using the force of unconscious will. Vivian moved to the bedside without speaking. They looked at each other in the dark room. The only light seeping in through the open window was from a half moon. It was almost as if Vivian was waiting to find out if Ida would invite her to stay or ask her to leave. At a loss for words, her heart thumping in her chest in anticipation, Ida pulled back the covers as an invitation. Vivian smiled broadly before taking off her shirt and climbing in next to Ida wearing only boxer-style shorts. They snuggled next to each other, lying on their sides so that they were facing each other, speaking in hushed voices.

"I thought you'd never come join me in here." Ida caressed Vivian's cheek.

"Sleeping in the next room, knowing that you are in here alone, is driving me crazy. I couldn't take it one more night."

"Me either."

"Will your leg be okay if we sleep together?"

"I doubt I'll notice the leg, assuming that you don't mean we'll actually sleep."

Vivian smiled again and leaned into Ida, covering her mouth with a passionate kiss, as she pulled their bodies closer together. "God, you feel so good."

"Hmm, so do you." Ida ran her fingers through Vivian's hair. Warm lips explored Ida's neck, down to her shoulders. Vivian pulled the strap of her nightgown aside and placed soft, affectionate kisses all along her collarbone. The sensation of being caressed so luxuriously by Vivian's lips elicited chills up and down her arms.

This somehow felt different from the nights they'd spent under the stars. Maybe it was the buildup of anticipation, or maybe it was that Ida felt closer to Vivian after her rescue from the trap. Whatever the reason, her emotional response to every touch from Vivian seemed heightened.

Ida moaned as Vivian slid down a little so that she could kiss one of Ida's breasts. Through the thin fabric, Vivian caressed her nipple with her tongue, sending a shock wave to the warm place between Ida's thighs. After a moment, Vivian slid back up to kiss Ida again on the lips while slowly stroking her breasts with her insistent fingers.

"Oh, God, Vivian..." Ida arched into Vivian, wanting more contact. Vivian pulled Ida's hips against her, centering one thigh between Ida's legs. Ida settled onto her back to give Vivian better access. Vivian moved partially on top of Ida, her heat and scent sending Ida's arousal even higher. Ida felt Vivian's fingers explore the hem of her nightgown, and Vivian moved her hand up inside the garment to caress the ever so slight, rounded shape of Ida's stomach at the space just before it plunged to the V between her thighs. She hesitated for a moment as if waiting to see if Ida would stop her. But this time Ida didn't stop Vivian as her hand traveled farther down to caress the sensitive place between her legs.

"If you want me to stop you need to say something now." Vivian pushed ever so gently against the spot where Ida most wanted to feel Vivian's strong fingers.

"I don't want you to stop." Ida pressed into Vivian's hand. "Please don't stop."

While Vivian caressed and teased, Ida kissed her fiercely, moving her hands over Vivian's broad muscular shoulders and back. God, she wanted this so badly. She craved the weight of Vivian on top of her, grounding her, making her feel safe and desired.

For a moment, Vivian moved her hand away from between Ida's legs, and in one upward motion, pulled the nightgown up high enough to expose Ida's breasts to her hot mouth. Vivian centered herself over Ida, kissing one breast and then the other, while holding Ida's arms pressed into the pillow above her head.

"I want to put my hands on you." Ida squirmed beneath her, so incredibly turned on that she feared she might reach orgasm without Vivian ever touching her.

"Not yet." Vivian trailed her tongue lightly down the center of Ida's chest. "I need a little more time...right here." Vivian paused her descent to kiss Ida low on her stomach.

"You're driving me crazy." She freed her arms enough to pull the nightgown over her head, leaving only her panties and Vivian's boxers to separate them.

For a moment, the frenzy slowed. Vivian slid up so that she could see Ida's face. The look she gave Ida was so intense and penetrating that she felt it slice through her chest like a sharp, hot blade.

"Ida, I want you so badly. I've wanted you for days now." Their lips collided in a deep kiss as she felt Vivian remove her panties. "I want to be inside. I want to feel how wet you are." Vivian murmured the words against Ida's cheek.

There would be no turning back if she didn't stop this now, which she had no intention of doing. She wanted to feel Vivian inside her, claiming her. She wanted to give herself over to Vivian completely. And so she did.

"Come for me, Ida. That's it."

"Yes, Vivian, oh…"

Ida felt Vivian's firm fingers inside, slowly at first. But as Ida's hips rose to meet each thrust, the rhythm and intensity increased. Ida buried her mouth into Vivian's neck so as not to scream out with Rebecca sleeping in the next room. She rocked under Vivian, taking more of her with each rocking motion until ecstasy exploded and her entire body shook. Vivian held her close until the tremors passed, pressing her full weight on top of her. As Ida settled, Vivian kissed her perspiring forehead.

"Don't move just yet." Ida wanted the moment to last.

"Was that okay?" There was such gentleness in Vivian's voice.

"Yes. Much better than okay." Ida caressed Vivian's back.

After a few minutes, Vivian pulled out slowly, and Ida felt the absence of their physical connection immediately. She wanted more.

She opened her eyes and looked up at Vivian with pure affection. Kissing her cheek and her jaw, Ida trailed her hands down Vivian's ribs until they found the top of her briefs and slowly pushed them down, past her pronounced hipbones.

"I want to feel you, Vivian. All of you." Vivian shifted, centered over Ida's thigh, so that Ida could place her hand between them. Ida watched Vivian's face as her eyes closed and her jaw clenched. She knew from touching her that she was as aroused as Ida had been just a few moments earlier. She pushed inside as Vivian began to move on top of her, bracing herself on her elbows to allow for more movement. As Vivian tightened around Ida's fingers she pulled Ida's other thigh up next to her hip and thrust into her again.

"I want to feel you again."

"Vivian, yes…" She was going to bring them both to climax. The sensation of being inside Vivian while Vivian was inside her was excruciatingly sensual. Vivian held fast as they came together in a rush. Only after the waves of orgasm subsided did Vivian allow Ida to pull out and she released her.

Ida was breathless and clinging to Vivian. "I've never felt anything like that." She worried that she'd dug the nails of her free hand into Vivian's back in the last seconds of orgasm. "Did I hurt you?"

"If you did, then please hurt me again in a few minutes." Vivian settled her head onto Ida's shoulder as she shifted her weight off to one side. "If I had known it would feel like this I would never have agreed to wait."

Ida kissed Vivian's forehead and caressed her hair. "You are incredible. Truly. A wildfire."

Vivian chuckled softly. "I knew I should never have told you my middle name. Now I'll never hear the end of it."

"No, you won't." Ida tilted Vivian's face up so that she could kiss her. "I'll let you rest for a little while, but then I'd like a little more of you." They snuggled close, and despite a mutual desire to make love again, they drifted off to sleep.

CHAPTER EIGHTEEN

Vivian thought she was dreaming, but then she realized the kisses were real. She fought to wake up. Her lids were heavy and her brain was foggy. But thanks to the sensation of Ida's delicate mouth on her skin, other parts of her body were wide-awake. At some point after they fell asleep, Vivian had rolled onto her back and now Ida was tenderly kissing her chest, taking special care to pay close attention to each breast as she made her way from one side to the other and slowly back again. Her hair fell across Vivian's chest and made feather-soft caresses across her bare skin every time Ida shifted her head from side to side. Ida smiled up at her when she realized Vivian was awake. The room was very dark. It was still nighttime, so they must have just dozed for a little while.

"Hey, come here." Vivian pulled Ida's soft warmth on top of her. She pulled Ida's hips firmly in place over hers and instantly registered how wet Ida was.

"I'm sorry. I woke up and there you were, right next to me."

"I'm glad I was here." Vivian placed a hand at the back of Ida's neck and pulled her down into a kiss. How had she managed to fall asleep with Ida lying next to her?

Ida departed from Vivian's lips, and slowly and seductively began to kiss her way down Vivian's body. Ida slid her hips between Vivian's thighs as she glided along her body, positioning herself just at the tip of Vivian's torso. Vivian moaned. Ida's mouth was so attentive Vivian's overly sensitive abdomen twitched with every sensuous brush of Ida's soft lips.

At the first contact of Ida's mouth at the apex of her thighs, Vivian seized a handful of Ida's hair, signaling for her to increase the pressure. Vivian couldn't keep still. She rocked her hips as Ida held her, keeping her mouth in constant contact with Vivian's aroused flesh.

"Ida, you're too far away. Come up here so I can touch you."

Ida stayed where she was, until the orgasm that had been building in Vivian subsided in shuddering quakes against Ida's mouth. Only then did Ida release her, crawling back up to rest her head on Vivian's chest. But she didn't get to relish that position for long. Vivian rolled her over on her side and cradled her body around Ida's. She pulled Ida's tousled hair aside and kissed the back of her neck, then her shoulders. Vivian was able to fondle Ida's breasts with one hand while Vivian's other hand caressed the sensitive skin along Ida's inner thigh.

"You woke me up; now you must suffer the consequences." She could tell Ida was smiling. She kissed Ida's cheek, her neck, and then pressed her front down to the bed so that she could kiss all along her back. Her back was milky and so receptive to Vivian's tongue. She traced the delicate contours of her shoulder blades with her lips.

Vivian lightly kissed the base of Ida's neck as she slid her hand slowly between Ida's legs and began to massage her.

"You're so wet." Vivian tried to go slow, to tease, but she couldn't resist pushing gently into Ida from behind. Ida moaned with pleasure. Her sounds partially muffled by the pillow near her face, as Vivian pressed into her back and hips. Vivian was going to come again just from the friction of moving her burning center against Ida as she rhythmically thrust in and out.

Ida reached her hand around and grabbed Vivian's hair. She was coming fast and hard.

"That's it, baby. I've got you."

"Oh, Vivian, oh—"

The orgasm claimed them both with force, and even after their breathing had returned to normal and the shuddering subsided, Vivian didn't move her hand. She wasn't ready to lose the bond between them. After a few moments, Ida twisted in her arms seeking Vivian's mouth. Vivian relinquished on command, slowly removing her fingers and allowing Ida to turn over to face her. They kissed tenderly and deeply.

As Vivian cradled Ida, she knew she was completely smitten. Ida had possessed her senses in a way she'd never experienced before. A feeling of vulnerability washed over her. She was emotionally exposed but she felt safe at the same time. This was a new experience for Vivian, and she wasn't sure she was ready for it.

CHAPTER NINETEEN

Ida yawned and stretched only to discover the space next to her in bed was empty. Light streamed through the open window indicating that she'd slept later than she intended. No doubt Vivian had woken up early, as was her habit, and left quietly, not wanting to wake her. Ida luxuriated for a few moments, rolling over and smelling the scent of Vivian on the pillow next to her. Still nude under the covers, she replayed their night together. Heat rose to her cheeks as she remembered the things they'd done. Things she was anxious to do again. Since when did she become so sex crazed? She had to smile at her circular train of thoughts as she dressed slowly, still mindful of her mending leg, which she had not thought of at all during the night.

When she stepped out of her room to the kitchen she was surprised to see Rebecca lingering there with coffee at such a late hour. It had to be way past eight in the morning. Rebecca greeted her with a smile and a playful tilt of her eyebrows as Ida reached to pour herself some coffee.

"Good morning." Ida added a bit of warm cream to her coffee. It was such a luxury to not only have coffee, but also fresh cream from the farm's cow.

"I'd say it's an even better morning for you." Rebecca tweaked an eyebrow.

"Oh, no, did we make that much noise last night?" Ida blushed furiously at the idea that Rebecca had heard them making love.

"You were quiet, but sounds travel in an all-wood house."

Ida groaned and covered her face with her hand.

"You're glowing, by the way. It's a good look for you." Rebecca pulled Ida's hand away from her face. "I'm happy that there is love in this house again. I think it's a good thing. Please don't feel embarrassed."

"I'll try not to, but I'm not sure that's possible." Ida sipped her coffee and moved away from the stove to settle into a chair at the table. She still had a slight limp, but her leg was feeling much stronger. "Did you see Vivian this morning?"

"Only for a moment. She was up very early. She said she was going turkey hunting." Rebecca took a seat opposite Ida. "A baked turkey would be a real treat."

"Did she blush as much as I just did?"

"No, but then again, I didn't let on that I knew anything had happened. She seemed lost in thought as she was leaving. I really only saw her for a minute before she headed out the door." Rebecca rested her arm on the table and placed her chin in her hand. "So, details. Please tell me details. Was it as amazing as it sounded?"

Ida groaned and laid her head on the table. "I thought you said we were quiet!"

❖

Vivian studied the turkey carcass lying prone by her foot. She'd been lucky and spotted the large tom turkey over an hour ago in the dim, early morning light. But instead of heading back to the farm, she'd settled next to a tree to think. She knew that the others would be grateful that she'd gone hunting for all of them. But she also knew that wasn't the real reason she'd roused herself at sunrise.

She'd woken with a start, a bad dream that she couldn't remember. The only lingering recollection she had from it was the feeling of being trapped. Ida's warm body next to her challenged all her senses. She was instantly aroused and at the same time frightened by what had transpired between them.

She realized that she cared enough about Ida to be really hurt by her. She wasn't sure she was ready to be in a situation where someone else had such power over her. She'd promised herself she wouldn't let this happen, but her desire for Ida was so strong that she'd given in. But this had been different from her time with Elizabeth. Something out of her control happened when she was with Ida. Something that made her want to let Ida into her heart for real. All the way in.

She'd fallen asleep feeling safe but had woken with doubts. Rather than linger for what she expected to be an awkward morning-after conversation, she'd decided to be alone to think. The excuse to go hunting hadn't presented itself to her until she'd run into Rebecca in the kitchen. No doubt Rebecca had a good idea of what had happened between her and Ida because she saw Vivian exit from Ida's room. Anyone would assume they slept together. She didn't relish a discussion with Rebecca first thing in the morning any more than she did with Ida, so she'd reached for her bow and made a quick escape. But now it was time to head back and clean the bird for its long bake.

Even in her youth, hunting had sometimes been her excuse to be alone. Her grandfather knew this and never offered to accompany her unless she specifically invited him. Usually time alone with trees would help her sort out whatever problem was bothering her. Something about the stoic silent sentinels, with roots buried deep and arms reaching skyward, invoked in Vivian's imagination the wisdom she assumed their fibers contained. As she'd slowly walked south from the farm she'd occasionally stopped and placed an open palm on an old growth maple or oak, hoping to get some spark of insight from its age-wizened vantage point. It was dumb luck that she spotted the turkey in the low brush ahead of her because hunting had been the last thing on her mind.

At some point during their stay at the farm, late summer had shifted to early fall. Dry leaves crackled under each boot fall as Vivian tromped back toward the road that would lead to Rebecca's homestead. The weather was still warm during the day, but nights were cooling as September had arrived and October waited on its heels.

When she got back to the farm, Vivian didn't go to the house right away. She decided to clean the turkey behind the barn on an old chopping block. When she finally delivered the bird to the house, only Rebecca was in sight. Ida was in the back of the house taking a bath. Relieved, Vivian handed the large bird over to Rebecca and made an excuse for leaving again. She'd seen some damaged fence railing down on the far side of the lower field when she was walking back.

Rebecca took the bird gratefully, but Vivian sensed that she could see something else was going on. Thankfully, Rebecca didn't ask. Vivian rationalized that she just needed a little more time to herself today to better understand what she was feeling. Her emotions were like rough water, tossing her about. One minute she'd be bathed in warm thoughts of Ida entwined with her in bed. The next, she'd have the cold ache of uncertainty. She should have just stayed in bed and talked with Ida. The longer she avoided her today, the more uncomfortable she would be. Her plan to gain some distance was only making her more confused about what was happening between them.

❖

Ida towel-dried her hair and walked out toward the front porch. Something good was baking in the oven. As she stepped outside, Rebecca was just coming back to the house with some potatoes.

"How does that turkey smell?" Rebecca asked.

"Great." Ida moved to the side so that Rebecca could use the steps to the porch. "I suppose that means Vivian is back. Is she here?"

"She was in and out. She said something about fixing one of the lower fences."

The news that Vivian came to the house and didn't even bother to say hello to her settled like a knot in Ida's stomach. She didn't want to be paranoid, but she was beginning to get the idea that Vivian was avoiding her. Why would she do that? Had something happened last night that bothered Vivian? Was she having regrets that they'd slept together? Ida wanted to talk to Vivian and sort things out. She hoped she was just being overly sensitive. Unfortunately, it would be another couple of hours before she could get her answers.

After helping Rebecca with laundry and putting a fresh pan of cornbread in to bake alongside the basting turkey, Ida stepped out of the house to look for Vivian. She found her in the barn sharpening arrow tips. Vivian looked up as she approached. Ida's first thought after closing the barn door was that Vivian looked sad.

"Hey," said Ida.

"Hey." Vivian stopped what she was doing and leaned against the workbench, facing Ida. There were two windows, one on each side of the barn. But they were small so they could be shuttered in bad weather. They cast very little light inside, especially at this late afternoon hour.

"I was hoping I'd see you this morning." Ida moved toward Vivian. Unable to read her body language, she was careful to give her some space.

"Yeah, sorry. I thought it would be good if I did a little hunting for us. I didn't want to wake you."

"But then you didn't come find me when you got back." It was hard for Ida not to reveal the hurt she was feeling in her voice. "Did I do something to upset you?"

"No. Why would you think that?" Vivian turned back toward her work and shifted items around on the bench.

"I don't know. I just wondered if you were avoiding me."

"Just because I didn't get a chance to hang out in the house today doesn't mean I'm avoiding you."

Vivian said the words, but to Ida, their meaning didn't match their tone. She wasn't going to let Vivian off the hook that easily. After making love the night before, like she'd never done with anyone, Ida thought she deserved more from Vivian than distance and attitude.

"I don't believe you. I think you were avoiding me, and I want to know why."

"You don't believe me? Why would I lie to you?" Vivian's voice was noticeably louder.

"I don't know. You tell me. Does this have something to do

with what you went through with Elizabeth?" Ida threw out a hunch, and quickly learned she'd hit a nerve.

"I'm sorry I ever told you about her. She has nothing to do with you and me. Nothing." Vivian gave Ida a stern look.

Ida ignored the end-of-discussion signal and pressed forward. "You said you weren't in love with her, so this must be about something else. What aren't you telling me?"

"Why do you assume there's anything to tell? We had sex. I was out all day. End of story. Don't make more of this than it is."

"We had sex?" And then in a louder voice. "We had sex?" Ida stepped closer so that she could more clearly see Vivian's face. "That, Vivian Yates, was not just sex. You know it and I know it. What happened between us last night was something bigger than just sex. You go ahead and try to minimize your feelings about it. But I was there. I felt you inside me." Ida was standing close to Vivian now, jabbing her forefinger into Vivian's chest. "I saw you, Vivian, really saw you. Don't pretend I didn't!"

As she said the last few words, angry tears began to trail down her cheeks. She was heartbroken that Vivian would make so little of what she thought they both had experienced the night before. It was as if the wind had been sucked from her lungs. She wiped at her tears. The last thing she wanted to do was cry in front of Vivian.

"You're a coward, Vivian Yates. My only regret is that I didn't see it sooner."

Ida turned away from her and made quick strides to the door. Vivian rushed to stop Ida's exit.

"Ida, wait—" But her plea was cut short. Her head was met with a heavy blow just as she stepped through the barn's threshold.

CHAPTER TWENTY

Vivian's eyes fluttered open. She knew instantly something wasn't right. The musty scent of saturated ground invaded her nostrils. The side of her face was against a sodden earth floor. Her head ached. Her movements were hindered. She discovered that her hands and feet had been bound by rope, and after another few minutes of gathering her senses, she reckoned that she'd been shut up inside the small springhouse near the barn. As her eyes adjusted to the barely visible moonlight seeping in around the edges of the plank door, she could make out the shelving stocked with canned vegetables in glass jars and the rough white oak baskets filled with potatoes by her feet.

Why was she in the springhouse? What happened? She remembered being with Ida in the barn. Ida was really upset. Then Ida ran away from her. And then a blinding, bone-jarring jolt struck the side of her head. If she was in here, where was Ida? This worried her more than she could consider at the moment. First order of business was to get out of the bindings. She got herself in a seated position and looked for any tool that might be used to cut through the ropes. Nothing presented itself. She usually carried a knife, but she hadn't had it while working on arrow tips in the barn.

After a moment, her gaze settled on the reflective surface of a glass jar of beans. Glass cuts and could cut rope. She just needed to figure out how to break one of the jars.

If she could kick one of the supports from under the shelving, maybe the fall would break one of the jars. More than one would have to fall to make her plan work as the damp dirt floor probably wasn't hard enough to break a single jar as it fell. Vivian lay on her back, and with both feet still tied together, she began to kick at the old rack near the door. Once, twice, ten times she kicked with all her might until finally she knocked the post loose and jars cascaded off the downwardly slanted shelf. Jars rolled and shattered near her feet as they fell one on top of another. The noise sounded deafening in the previously silent space.

Vivian sat still for a moment listening for any footsteps that her clamor might have called forth. When none came, she set about searching for a shard of glass large enough for her to hold and work it through the strands of the thick twine around her wrists. Once she scooted around and got her hands on such a piece, the task of cutting seemed to take forever. She had also cut her hands in the searching for and working of the shard. The sticky warmth of her blood gathered in her dirty palms.

When she finally loosened her hands, she reached down to free her feet. Feeling suddenly woozy, she felt along the side of her face. Blood, both dried and wet, seeped from a cut on her forehead. She stood up, swaying, and moved in the small dark space toward the door, which to her surprise wasn't latched.

Vivian had no idea how long she'd been unconscious, or who had hit her. But her heightened senses told her to exercise caution. Only when she was outside the small stone springhouse and slipping silently along the shadowed side of the barn did she hear laughter coming from the open windows of the main house. It was a man's laughter. Near the other side of the barn a horse hitched to a wagon stood munching the low grass of the front lawn. Several loud, indecipherable masculine voices now emitted from the windows. Vivian decided to move closer to the house for a better look.

She scurried to one of the side windows and eased up just enough past the windowsill to get a quick view of who was inside. Two men. One was standing next to the table, next to Ida! He roughly shoved Ida and raised one of the kitchen chairs over his head to slam it onto the floor. The sight of anyone touching Ida in such a rough manner made Vivian furious. When the chair didn't break, the man used it to swipe the entire table, sending dishes neatly arranged for the evening meal cascading against the far wall in a symphony of broken glass. He threw the unbroken chair across the room, barely missing Rebecca, who was seated on the floor.

Vivian ducked again and, after a moment, gave another quick look. This time she spotted a second man with a club standing across the room, laughing at the antics of his partner. He must have been the one who hit her as she was leaving the barn. She never saw him as she stepped through the door. *What's that?* Movement caught Vivian's eye and she saw that there was also a young boy in the room, standing apart from the others.

Vivian took the whole situation in. She knew Ida and Rebecca were not safe, and that she needed to figure out some way to intervene. She fought off the nausea that threatened to rise as she imagined what these men might do to Ida. Rage thumped in her chest. No one would harm Ida, not while she was still breathing.

It was a mystery and a blessing that the two men had seen her as more of a threat than the others and had chosen to separate her. Now she just needed to use that to her advantage.

From her crouched position under the window, she overheard one of the men say loudly, "Boy, go fetch us a bottle from the wagon. We're celebrating tonight! And, woman, get us some food!"

Vivian heard footsteps on the plank floor of the porch. She saw a small figure move across the front lawn toward the wagon. She was on him quickly. With a hand over the boy's mouth, she pulled him behind the wagon out of sight.

"Don't be afraid. I'm not going to hurt you," Vivian whispered. "I'll move my hand if you'll be quiet. Do you understand?"

The boy nodded, and she removed her hand. Somehow she had known that the boy was not family to these men. Maybe it was the tone of the man's voice as he commanded the boy to do his bidding.

"I'm Vivian. What's your name?"

"Peter."

"Peter, are these men friends of yours?"

The boy shook his head.

"Have they hurt you?"

"Only a little. When I don't do things fast enough, they hit me. They hurt my dad real bad. He never got up after that." Tears welled up in his eyes. "They'll hurt your friends, too. I'm sure of it."

"So am I," said Vivian. She was kneeling beside the boy who looked to be no more than eight or nine years old. He had sandy hair and she could make out freckles even through the dirt smeared on his face. The two of them didn't make the most intimidating pair, but they had surprise on their side, and Vivian planned to use that.

Plus, earlier that day, Vivian had managed to fashion some new flint tips for arrows. Her bow, and a small supply of newly minted shafts, waited for her just inside the barn. She had the start of a plan, but she would need Peter's help for the execution.

Chapter Twenty-one

Ida cried out as the man shoved her toward the wall. She banged her thigh on the side of the kitchen table as she weaved and stumbled. This man's smell was as rank as his temperament. Unfortunately, he was much larger than she was so he easily overwhelmed her attempts to dodge his blows. She felt with her hand the spot on her cheek where he'd struck her. What was going to happen to them? Where was Vivian, and was she okay? These questions swam in her head as she leaned against the kitchen wall, attempting to shrink away from his chaotic swings with a chair that he now held aloft.

He had ordered the boy to go outside to fetch booze from the wagon, and now he motioned toward the pot on the stove. He and his friend had already eaten one huge serving each of the turkey that had cooked all afternoon. Now shards of those plates were scattered all about the kitchen floor. Ida moved cautiously toward a cabinet to retrieve a clean dish, all the while chancing a glance over her shoulder in Rebecca's direction. Rebecca was still on the floor.

Ida had been so angry and upset when she fled the barn. Her eyes so full of tears that she'd run right into the arms of one of the men who'd been patiently waiting outside. In the split second after she'd realized what was about to happen, the other man swung at Vivian in mid sprint. She'd gone down hard, blood slowly streaming from a cut at the side of her brow. Ida struggled to look back at Vivian as she was dragged toward the house. She screamed Vivian's name, but Vivian didn't stir. The club-wielding intruder had remained, standing over Vivian's body waiting for the same sign of life.

Once in the house, Ida screamed at Rebecca to run, but it was too late. The man held Ida with one hand and swung at Rebecca with the other, sending her tumbling to the floor. The man left Rebecca crying on the floor and demanded food, which Ida quickly fetched for him. Shortly, the second man entered the main room, dragging a small boy behind him by the arm.

"You stand there and don't move!" the man barked at him.

Rebecca had managed to slide far enough on the floor so that she was sitting up with her back against the wall. The young boy stood sheepishly above her, his eyes cast downward.

The man who brought the boy in dragged Rebecca to one of the upholstered chairs close to the hearth. He settled himself in the twin armchair to her left.

Ida didn't like the look of either of the men. The malice in their leers was like a physical presence in the room bearing down on them. As Ida approached with the second serving for the man who seemed to be the leader, he snatched the bowl out of her hand and slapped her across her mouth, sending her reeling to the floor. Despite the pain, Ida quickly looked back at the man. And then it came to her, as if he'd shaken the memory loose when he hit her. This man was the same man she'd glimpsed from the cover of the Franklins' wagon. The man with the long scar on his face.

With his mouth full, he turned and shouted loud enough for the boy to hear him from outside. "What's taking so long, boy!"

Then he noticed that Ida was staring at him. "What are you lookin' at?" He punctuated his question by kicking her with his boot.

❖

Vivian coaxed Peter to return to the house without the bottle of booze so that he could ask one of the men to come outside and help him find it.

"I'm counting on you to be brave, Peter. I know you can do this." Vivian kneeled in front of the frightened child, resting her hands on his shoulders. "I'll be right here when you come back. I won't let him hurt you."

The boy nodded and walked into the house. Vivian heard loud, angry, muffled voices before she saw a large hulking figure follow the boy out of the house and across the open space toward the wagon where Vivian stood waiting just out of view. The wagon was built for storing and transporting goods. Its sides were converted into tall cabinets, and she was easily hidden from view behind them.

The man gruffly shoved the boy as he rounded the wagon. "Out of my way, boy! I'll get the damn whiskey. I don't know why I have to—" His reprimands were cut short by the sight of Vivian standing ten feet away with her poised bow arm outstretched. Its string was taut.

The man reached to pull his knife, but the blade hadn't cleared the sheath when Vivian loosened the shaft that struck him square in the center of his chest. He fell back like a heavy stone. She swiftly moved to his side as a gurgling sound emitted from his throat, along with a splattering of blood as he tried to speak. Vivian felt no pity for such a creature as this. Who would kidnap a young boy, and do God knows what else when left to his own base inclinations? She took the blade from his limp hand and forced it between his ribs and into his heart. This was no less than what she would have done for a badly wounded deer. But she would have felt more remorse for the deer.

The boy sat frozen on the ground where he'd fallen after the man had pushed him. His eyes were wide as he stared at the knife protruding like a gleaming steel tombstone from its burial in the man's chest.

"Peter." Vivian spoke softly as she moved to kneel beside him. "Don't be afraid. This man would have killed me first if he'd been given the chance."

The boy nodded and slowly looked away from the still figure to meet Vivian's gaze. "I know," he said.

"Listen to me. You've done your share here. I'm going into the house to finish this, and I want you to stay out here where it's safe." Vivian brushed the sticky strands of hair from his forehead and tried to give him a weak smile. "If I don't come back in a few minutes, you run and hide. Do not stay here. Do you hear me?"

"Yes. But come back, okay?"

She smiled down at him. "I plan on it."

Vivian stood studying the house's exterior for a moment. She bent to retrieve the knife from the body near her feet and slipped its still bloodied blade under her belt. She adjusted the strap for the quiver over her chest and pulled a fresh arrow free, holding it downward, loosely against the bow. Vivian gave the boy one more reassuring look before she strode through the dark. She urged herself to push through her fear of what awaited on the other side of the home's entryway. If she discovered that Ida had been injured in any way while she'd been tied up in the springhouse, she wouldn't be responsible for the wrath she would unleash on the man inside.

Silently, Vivian moved into the main living space. The lantern light danced eerily around the walls of the great room as a breeze from an open window pushed past. Vivian didn't speak and she didn't meet Ida's wide-eyed gaze. She focused all her attention on the man seated at the table. She wouldn't kill a man who wasn't facing her, even a low-life mongrel such as this one. She didn't have to wait long for him to sense her presence.

The man slowly pivoted his head as if he'd become aware that Ida, still on the floor near his feet, was no longer looking at him. His gaze followed Ida's until he settled on Vivian standing just inside the doorway with her taut bow in hand.

He stood to face Vivian as if to measure her threat. Vivian carried the bloodied knife at her waist, and the side of her face felt sticky and warm from the blood that still drained slowly from the wound on her head.

The man looked as if he wanted to say something. But as she raised the bow, the words never came. He pulled Ida up and in front of him, poising his hunting knife at her side. He clutched her delicate throat with no remorse.

"Drop the weapon, girl," the man commanded. He spat the words over Ida's shoulder as he used her as a shield.

The man was wrong to doubt Vivian's marksmanship. She didn't obey his request or respond verbally. She didn't hesitate to see what his next move or taunt might be. Vivian released the arrow, and it struck through his left eye, just passing the side of Ida's face. The man uttered a strangled sound as he dropped to his knees, falling sideways away from where Ida stood.

The boy, who hadn't done as he was told, ran from where he'd been watching just outside the open door and hugged Vivian around the waist. She looked down at the small creature clinging to her. She had the sensation of having just been released from some dark trance. She placed her hand on Peter's back to comfort him. Vivian turned to meet Ida's shocked gaze, her eyes filled with unshed tears.

CHAPTER TWENTY-TWO

They had dragged the bodies outside and burned them as far away from the barn and house as they could manage. Vivian tossed onto the burial pyre the kitchen chair that had been broken by the man's unexplained rage. Ida swept up the broken dishes from around the table. Rebecca fed the boy, who seemed nearly starved.

Vivian watched with an unfocused stare into the blaze until Ida returned to bring her into the house. Vivian had cleared the debris and had made a fire ring of sorts so what remained of the flame wouldn't present a danger and could be left untended.

Vivian looked down as she felt Ida's fingers slip between hers.

"Come into the house, Vivian."

Vivian didn't speak. She only nodded as she allowed herself to be led inside, where Ida pushed her into one of the chairs around the kitchen table. Rebecca was seated nearby with her elbows on the table, her head in her hands. She had made some evening tea for herself and the others after settling the boy in to sleep on the pile of blankets in the main room near the fireplace, the place that Vivian had occupied when she first arrived at the farm. Ida brought a basin filled with water to the table and sat facing Vivian. She gently dampened a clean cloth and wiped at the blood smeared down the side of Vivian's face.

As she tenderly cleaned Vivian's wound, Ida knew that they were destined to be lovers. Whatever it was that existed between them was too strong. It had been folly to think otherwise. Ida now knew that for however long this could last, whether long or short in time, she would have to give herself over to it. She regarded the wild darkness in Vivian's eyes as she brushed her thick black hair away from her forehead. She knew Vivian was looking at her, but not seeing her. Ida needed to bring Vivian back from whatever dark place she'd traveled to in order to do what she'd just done. Tenderly, Ida pressed her lips to Vivian's for a few moments then pulled away. Vivian's gaze seemed to shift focus, and Ida sensed the tension lessen in Vivian's body.

Vivian looked down and saw the feathery tendrils of red swirling about in the basin. She'd forgotten about the wound on her head. Adrenaline seemed to have kept her head from pounding from the injury. As Ida continued to clean her wound, Vivian winced as if she'd just that minute returned to take up residence in her own body. She also finally noticed the bruise on Ida's cheek.

Vivian reached to brush the back of her fingers across the bruise only to become aware of how black and dirty her hand was from soot and dried blood. She turned her hand over and studied it as if it belonged to someone else.

"Why don't we draw a bath? You'll feel better after," Ida said.

"I must look pretty scary at the moment." Vivian looked down at her torn and soiled clothing.

"You look like a warrior." Rebecca spoke for the first time since Vivian sat down. "And for that, I am grateful."

Vivian smiled weakly at Rebecca, exhausted, but at the same time relieved that they were all safe. She looked over to where the boy lay sleeping. She hoped what she had done would in some way right the sad path his short life had taken.

Ida excused herself and filled the claw-foot tub with cool water. She used the still-hot water from the kettle to top it off and helped Vivian shuck her garments and sink into the soothing warmth. Ida closed the door behind them before she disrobed and slipped into the tub behind Vivian. They had never bathed together, and while under different circumstances this might have been incredibly erotic, at that moment, what they both needed was solace.

Vivian sank back into Ida's embrace, allowing herself to be comforted as they washed the remnants of the day from each other's skin. Ida lightly wiped at the cuts and scrapes around her wrists from the ropes and the broken glass shards she'd used to sever them. As Vivian lingered in Ida's nurturing arms, she allowed herself to reflect on the events of the past few weeks. She had experienced things and done things that she could not have imagined. Vivian pulled Ida's hand to her mouth and kissed it with reverence before settling it down over the hollow space above her heart.

"Ida, I'm so sorry about how I acted earlier today. You didn't deserve that."

Ida kissed her temple. "Shh, it's okay. We don't have to talk about that now."

"You were right. I was being a coward." Vivian shifted to the side a little so that she could see Ida's face. "When I thought I might lose you, I regretted everything I hadn't said to you."

"Sweetheart, you are many things, but a coward is not one of them. I should never have said that to you. I was angry." Ida kissed Vivian's forehead. "We have time to talk later. For now, just rest."

Vivian settled against Ida's soft chest. "Okay." She knew there was more she needed to say, but those things could wait.

CHAPTER TWENTY-THREE

The next morning, Vivian stood near the remnants of their once smoldering bonfire. All that remained were black shards of things previously alive—trees and men. She had risen before the others, poring over the map she hadn't removed from her pack in many days. Vivian studied the notations and reasoned that, barring unforeseen obstacles or delays, they could reach the Blue Mountains in eight days. Had she subconsciously known she was that close and lingered out of fear? Meeting one's destiny was terrifying. She dismissed the notion, knowing they had lingered to give Ida time to heal.

Footsteps approached from behind. Vivian turned to greet Ida, who had a cup of coffee in hand for each of them. Vivian accepted her steaming mug gratefully.

"There was coffee in the wagon. I thought we might as well have some."

"I think that wagon is Rebecca's now, especially if the boy stays here with her." Vivian paused for a moment to take a few sips before continuing. "She will let him stay here, won't she?"

"Yes, of course. We lost one evening to those bastards. He lost his father and whatever life he had before this."

They stood side by side, looking away from the smoking rubble toward the barn and the field that lay beyond. The horse, unhitched from its wagon, was slowly circling the fence in search of fresh blades of grass.

"Are you ready to leave, Ida?" Vivian asked as she brushed the back of her hand ever so lightly over the bruise on Ida's cheek. "Does it hurt?"

Ida smiled, taking Vivian's hand in hers, and pressing her open palm against her lips. She closed her eyes, allowing herself this extended moment to be committed to memory. All of it: the smell of Vivian's skin, the brightness of the early light waking up a cloudless sky, the smell of dry hay wafting from the field, and the fondness in her heart.

They hadn't revisited the argument from the previous day. Instead, they had bathed together, and gone to bed nestled in the safety of each other's arms. She knew now that they would be together until they reached the mountains. Beyond that, she could not see.

Once they made the decision to leave, they decided not to draw out their departure. As soon as everyone had eaten breakfast, they gathered on the front stoop to say good-bye. Rebecca had filled Vivian's and Ida's satchels with as much food as she could, including a fair ration of coffee. Although they hadn't discussed it at great length, Vivian knew the boy would remain. She was happy to know Rebecca would no longer be alone. She needed Peter, and Peter needed her.

As they prepared to leave, Vivian spoke with Peter. She regarded the boy with seriousness as he stood close enough to Rebecca that his shirtsleeve brushed against the loose material of her flowing, knee-length skirt.

"Peter, do you know what your name means?" Vivian spoke quietly to him, balanced on one knee to be on his eye level.

He shook his head.

"In the old language, in the old book, Peter means *the Rock*." Vivian placed a hand on his shoulder to emphasize her words. "The rock that can withstand all manner of assault. The rock, upon which things are broken while it remains firm. The rock, upon which good things are built." She brushed the hair away from his forehead affectionately. "Be the rock, Peter."

Peter closed the space between them. Vivian wrapped her arms tightly around his little body. "You saved us, Peter."

As they released each other, Vivian kept her hands on his arms and looked him in the eye. "Take care of Rebecca for me, okay?"

Peter nodded, smiling.

As Ida released Rebecca from a warm embrace, Vivian turned to do the same. She pulled Rebecca into her arms. "Thank you for sheltering us when we really needed it." As she pulled back, tears glistened on Rebecca's cheeks.

"I will miss you both. Please take care of yourselves." Rebecca looked down and pulled Peter close. "Who knows, maybe we will see you both again sometime."

"I hope so," said Ida.

Vivian hoisted her pack, shouldered her bow, and then reached for Ida's hand as they walked away from the porch together toward the front gate. Vivian sensed that things were about to change for them. Whether this was a deliberate joining of fates or not, Vivian felt one emotion more than any other as they walked through the gate and turned east: hope.

CHAPTER TWENTY-FOUR

There were few signs of human habitation in the miles after they crossed into the territory known as Georgia. Vivian decided they should head north of whatever village she expected to find at the intersection of the main road and the Tombigbee River. Ida let Vivian direct their route since she'd spent the most time studying her grandfather's map.

Dams to the north had long since given way and so the river ran wide and shallow. They were able to swim and wade across without any real difficulty. After crossing the waterway, the terrain began to become hilly with the occasional granite outcropping. They walked among hardwoods covered at their roots by lush fern beds, occasionally passing through sections of the forest where kudzu, left unchecked, had swallowed entire groves.

On the evening of the third day after leaving Rebecca's farm, Vivian sat by the flames of their small campfire as she rummaged through her satchel for the last of the cornbread Rebecca had packed for them. After she pulled out the snack, Vivian realized she was within days of reaching her goal and arriving at the Blue Mountains. The truth of it was that she wasn't sure what she planned to do when she got there. Maybe on some level she never believed she'd actually make it that far. These thoughts stirred up a small whirl of self-doubt. Had she really been unhappy in Oklahoma? Had she made a mistake in leaving? Why could she not just settle down and be satisfied? Did she really have a destiny?

While walking these past few days, Vivian had reflected on the pieces of herself she'd left along the way: her ability to trust at the Hudson Ranch, her naivety at the Mississippi River, and her innocence that terrible night on Rebecca's farm. She had killed two men and carried no regrets. What sort of person was she going to be when she finally arrived in the Blue Mountains? Vivian sensed that Ida was studying her and looked across the flames to meet her watchful eyes.

"What were you thinking just now?" asked Ida.

"Truthfully?"

"Of course."

"I was wondering what will happen after I reach the mountains." Vivian handed half the cornbread across to Ida and slouched back into her seated position.

"What do you mean?"

"Well, I guess a part of me thought that reaching the mountains was such a long shot that I never bothered to figure out what I'd do once I arrived."

Ida watched Vivian's face to try to discern what Vivian felt about what she was saying. Ida had wondered the same thing but hadn't asked. Secretly, she wanted Vivian to stay with her at the farm. She wanted the chance for them to have a normal courtship and to see where things might take them. Ida decided to take a chance.

"I think part of me hoped you might stay on with me at the farm." Ida spoke quietly, as if speaking softly might be less frightening for both of them.

"Really? You thought that? Even after the way I acted that day in Rebecca's barn?"

"I did." Ida still wasn't sure what had really happened that day.

"You didn't say anything about me staying with you."

"I know." Ida looked down at the food in her hand. "I guess I was afraid you might think it was too soon to consider something more serious." She met Vivian's eyes again. "But the truth is, Vivian, I would like a chance to be with you. Not just out of necessity but because we choose to be with each other. I'd like the chance to see if we have a future."

Vivian didn't respond right away, which made Ida's stomach sink. She'd said too much.

"I would like that."

"You would?"

"I would." Vivian moved around the fire to sit close to Ida, facing her. "At least for a while, if it's really okay with you."

"Oh, Vivian." Ida stroked the side of Vivian's face with the palm of her hand. "Sweetheart." She leaned over and kissed Vivian tenderly. "Stay with me. At least long enough to give us a chance."

"If I do stay, I think I owe you an explanation for what happened that day in the barn." Vivian settled back, sitting cross-legged in front of Ida. "You were right. I was avoiding you that day." Vivian cleared her throat. "I think...I think I have a hard time allowing people to get close. No, that's not the complete truth. I chose not to let you get close and when we made love I realized I couldn't keep you distant from me. I was scared of what that meant."

Ida sat quietly eating, waiting for Vivian to continue.

"You asked if Elizabeth was the reason. I think I've been blaming Elizabeth, but I think it goes back further than that."

"Is it because of your mother?"

Vivian's eyes darted in shocked surprise. "What? Why would you say that?"

"Because you've never once mentioned her in the entire time we've traveled together. When talking about your childhood, you only ever mention your grandfather."

"I never talk about my mother. Ever." Vivian picked up a stick and began sketching shapes in the dirt near the fire ring.

"Is she dead?"

"Who knows?" Vivian stood and began pacing. "She left me with my grandfather when I was six months old and never came back." She stopped moving for a moment to peek back at Ida. "I don't even know who my father was. I guess some drifter."

Ida quickly went to Vivian, pulling her into a hug. "It's not your fault that your mother left. I'm so sorry."

Vivian returned the embrace, burying her face in Ida's hair. "I've never told anyone about my mother before you. I think

I've tried to pretend she never existed." Vivian pulled Ida closer, breathing her in. "It's the unanswered question that haunts me. The not knowing why."

Ida took Vivian's face between her hands so that she could look into her eyes. "Don't let an unanswered question define you, Vivian. You're so much more than where you came from or who your parents are. You're making your own destiny."

"You think so?"

"I do. With conviction."

Maybe Vivian had no vision beyond arriving at her destination because when she set out on her journey fate hadn't yet introduced her to Ida. It continually surprised Vivian how good Ida made her feel. Not just when they made love but in even the smallest caress or embrace. Previous physical acts and sexual encounters with other women felt like they took something away from her, an intangible siphoning of emotional capital. Intimacy with Ida was different; there was a giving rather than a taking away. Vivian felt more whole every time she was with Ida.

"I'm so glad you talked to me about this." Ida rested her cheek on Vivian's chest. "Let's just promise each other that the next time we get scared we'll talk it out."

"Sometimes you just have to say the things that matter," said Vivian.

Ida laughed at hearing her own advice delivered back to her. "Yes, someone wise must have said that."

"Very wise. And beautiful." Vivian kissed Ida. They kept kissing, their dinner forgotten for the moment as their bodies connected in a lingering hug by their fire.

CHAPTER TWENTY-FIVE

The next day, the rain began and did not stop. They were forced to huddle under a large granite overhang to get a brief reprieve. The downpour had soaked them to the bone. Building a fire was nearly impossible so they wrapped themselves in the damp blankets they had and huddled close to maximize their body heat. None of the food they'd carried from Rebecca's farm remained except for a small pouch of coffee. Vivian sensed that they were close to the next obstacle of their odyssey, the Chattahoochee River. She wasn't interested in attempting its crossing at night. They would sleep and try the river in daylight. Hopefully by then the rain would let up.

Vivian slept fitfully. In addition to hunger and exhaustion, she was chilled and couldn't get comfortable enough to sleep soundly. When she opened her eyes to the cloud-shrouded morning, Vivian saw that it was still raining. She decided the best way for them to warm up was to just start walking. Maybe the weather would clear if they kept working their way east.

After an hour of trekking, Vivian heard the sound of rushing water. The river was just ahead. The pathway leading toward the river was clear and well traveled. But the bank of the river was hidden by thick greenery. Lush plant life gathered near the moving water, creating a thick buffer that hid the river from clear view until they were standing right at its edge.

Unlike the previous water crossings, it appeared that someone had gone to considerable trouble to partially maintain the Chattahoochee River's ancient bridge. In the year of its creation, the bridge had no doubt been much wider. But over time, it had been patched and pieced with just the bare essentials, making the bridge now nothing more than a rickety foot passage.

Vivian surveyed the expanse of the overpass and leaned over to see the muddy, swirling torrent that passed under the crossing thirty feet below. Two days of rain had swollen the river, creating a speed and current far too daunting to dare swimming. Vivian stepped back from the suspended passageway's edge.

"Do you think it's safe?" asked Ida.

"I don't know. Something about this seems off." Vivian took another step back and surveyed the banks north and south of their position. "If someone was going to go to the trouble of maintaining a crossing like this, wouldn't they work the boundaries to charge some barter fee for passage?" The fact that there were no signs of life anywhere near the bridge gave Vivian pause.

"It does seem like they would. Maybe they just aren't here at the moment because of the weather."

The rain continued to fall in a steady stream as Vivian approached the edge of the waterway again, considering their options.

"Well, we can't swim it. I suppose we have no choice but to use the footbridge."

Vivian set out first on the narrow conduit. Rough boards were placed loosely over exposed, rusted rebar. The boards had been tied down with makeshift cord. A single, thick rope had been strung along each side of the footbridge to be used as a handrail. Vivian was careful to step near the center of each plank, testing the solidity of each before putting her full weight on the crosspieces. "Watch where I put my feet and follow my steps, okay?"

Ida nodded as she gingerly stepped out to follow, looking down through the spaces between each slat at the roaring muddy water beneath them.

Vivian concentrated on her footing, which was made even more difficult by the rain now falling in torrential sheets driven by a strengthened wind. These distractions kept her attention focused on the footbridge rather than on the riverbank in front of them. As Vivian peered ahead, she wiped a hand across her face to clear her vision. She now saw two dark figures. Vivian turned to look back only to find other dark figures standing in the spot they'd just left. Her stomach clinched. *Damn.* This crossing was obviously a trap, and in their hunger and fatigue they had stepped right into it. *But now what?* Vivian needed to consider options quickly. She wasn't about to allow them to be captured, or worse.

Ida stopped and looked up to see why they were no longer moving. Vivian took a half step back, placing a protective hand on Ida's arm to indicate she should stand still. Anger, which seemed to be hovering just beneath the surface ever since Elizabeth's betrayal, surged in Vivian's chest. After everything she'd been through, Vivian wasn't going to allow her journey to get derailed by an ambush. She checked both directions quickly. Neither group had stepped onto the bridge. They held their positions. *What are they waiting for?* There was no way she could take multiple assailants in a fight. She considered drawing her bow, but her footing was tenuous and visibility was terrible. Plus, taking a defensive stance would only make Ida an unarmed target. There was also the wind, which would make accuracy a challenge. They would have to jump and risk the current, or stay and risk possibly losing their lives.

Vivian gripped the rope lines tightly and looked down to measure the drop for a jump. Before she had time to fully consider the distance she felt a sharp pain strike her right shoulder. The arrow knocked her off balance, causing her foot to slip through a ragged opening between the slats. She fought to free her boot. Ida moved forward in an attempt to help her.

"Go! Jump!" Vivian grabbed Ida's arm for emphasis. "Jump!"

"Not without you!"

"Go! Now! I'm right behind you!"

Luckily, the second arrow sailed past without finding its mark. But they both saw it.

"Go!" Vivian shouted.

As soon as Ida plunged into the fast-moving water, Vivian struggled to get to her feet so that she could better control her dismount from the bridge. But before she could do that, the vibrations of multiple boots hit the footbridge from both sides. No time for a controlled leap. Vivian swung out on the rope line. Her freshly injured shoulder gave way, leaving her to drop into the raging water in an uncontrolled tumble.

The current was so fast that she was swiftly swept away from the surprise attack. In the murky, rain-swollen river she had to concentrate to figure out which way was up. When she surfaced she searched frantically for Ida. She heard muffled shouts from the direction of the bridge as she felt herself carried downstream. Vivian could also feel the shaft of the arrow still in her upper arm. She made an attempt to grab the wooden staff but realized she needed both arms moving to keep her head above water. The pack she still carried was filling with water, morphing into an anchor. It was several minutes before she managed to make any movement toward the eastern side of the river. There was rubble all along the bank, rock, weathered wood strips, even rusted pipe shards. It seemed nearly impossible to find a clear spot to approach land. And then she felt someone grab her from behind.

❖

Ida thought if she could just get close enough to the riverbank, she'd be able to grab a dangling branch and pull herself ashore. After struggling to cross the current for what seemed like an eternity, Ida finally got hold of a low-hanging bough strong enough to secure herself against the raging current. She looked for Vivian and found her traveling full-speed in her direction. Ida inched toward the muddy, overgrown riverbank, pulling Vivian behind her. But before they could get their footing, the bough gave way, tossing them back into the undertow.

Ida kept her grip on Vivian's uninjured arm as the current spun them along the river's edge. Vivian managed to reach for a partially submerged limb to stop their downstream free fall.

"You first!" Vivian shouted over the roar of the water.

Ida, clinging to Vivian's shirt, pulled herself around Vivian and up onto the bank. She turned and helped Vivian, who was struggling with her wounded shoulder. After heaving themselves up onto shore, they collapsed under heavy shrubbery. The packs they'd been carrying were completely soaked, doubling their weight. Ida dropped hers then tried to ease Vivian's off her shoulder, but the narrow rod of the arrow shaft made the second strap hard to remove. Ida unbuckled the leather fastener and let the pack fall to the ground. While listening for signs of the men from the bridge, Ida examined Vivian's wound. The wooden shaft of the arrow had broken off midway. No doubt it had been impacted by the river's strong current and debris. The force of the blow had also further torn the entry wound. Ida reasoned that this might make it easier for her to pull the arrow point free.

Ida met Vivian's pained gaze. "We need to get this out of your arm."

Vivian nodded.

Vivian placed the free end of the leather strap from her pack between her teeth and bit down. She nodded for Ida to do her work. They couldn't afford to make any noise and risk giving away their location. Vivian clenched her teeth against the damp leather, and Ida tugged with all her might. As the stone tip pulled free, ripping her tender flesh, Vivian doubled over with pain. Blood ran down her arm, soaking her water-logged sleeve.

Ida pulled Vivian's face against her chest. "I'm so sorry. I know that hurt," she said. "I'm so sorry."

Ida started from the hole the weapon had made and ripped the rest of the shirtsleeve free. She tied the strip of fabric as tightly as possible around Vivian's wound to slow the bleeding. After that task was complete, Vivian collapsed. Using one of the soggy packs as a pillow, Ida cushioned Vivian's head, and they huddled under the thick, wet tent of shrubbery and allowed exhaustion to claim them.

❖

Muffled voices jerked Vivian awake. Her head felt fuzzy and she was unsure of the time. The rain had slowed to a drizzle. Ida stirred beside her, and Vivian put a finger to her lips for Ida to remain silent. She listened for the voices she'd just heard.

"There's no sign of the bodies." It was a man's voice.

"Well, the river was moving pretty fast. If you'd been a better shot we wouldn't have this problem," said a different man.

"Regardless of my shot, we'd still likely be fishing a body out of the river. The rain made the bridge slick. We should have just waited until they were closer to the bank."

"Woulda, shoulda, coulda. It's too late now regardless."

The voices seemed to be heading north.

"At least the rain is slowing up."

There was one more muffled comment that Vivian couldn't make out as the two men continued walking northward away from their hiding spot. They must have passed just at the crest of the riverbank above. Vivian suggested that they wait until dusk to move. That would give them enough time to make sure no others lurked about searching for signs that they'd made it out of the river.

Ida shivered next to Vivian, who pulled her close. Their clothes had no chance of drying. Ida's teeth chattered and Vivian's shoulder throbbed. Vivian was also feeling extremely hungry and thirsty. She fished out a glass jar partially filled with water, drank half, and gave the rest to Ida. Her hunger would have to wait until they put some distance between themselves and the river.

❖

The rain finally stopped as sunset neared. The shadows were growing long when Vivian and Ida quietly climbed the steep bank to get a better idea of their position. Vivian was unsure of just how far they'd floated south before extracting themselves from the muddy torrent. Maybe a half mile? Maybe more. At any rate, they were now far south of the dirt path they'd been following east. They would need to find their way through the forest until they were at a safe enough distance to turn north and try to rejoin the roadway.

The position of the sun was low on the horizon. Vivian could just glimpse it through the humid haze of the damp forest grove. She used her uninjured arm to bring Ida close so she could plant a kiss on her temple. Ida's skin still felt cool and damp. "Are you okay?"

"I should be asking you that. How's your arm?"

"It hurts, but I can move it. So that's good news." Vivian smiled weakly at Ida. "That was pretty scary. A close call. Thank you for pulling us to the bank."

"Thank me? I never even saw those men at the edge of the bridge. If you hadn't seen them, I don't know what might have happened." Vivian felt Ida shudder and pressed her lips on Ida's wet hair. The truth was the entire event had scared her badly. She felt they were lucky to be alive and walking.

"Let's keep moving. That'll help warm us up."

Ida nodded.

They began walking east, keeping the sinking sun at their backs. An hour into their trek, they stumbled into a blackberry patch and picked a few handfuls for dinner. What they really needed was some protein, but Vivian didn't think they were far enough from the river to build a fire to cook game. More substantial food would have to wait.

As darkness descended, Vivian found a spot protected on three sides by large granite boulders. They could get some rest there and only have to worry about a stranger approaching from one direction.

Chapter Twenty-six

As soon as Ida roused herself from sleep, she realized something wasn't right. Her head hurt and her body had small aches everywhere, but that wasn't what worried her. Vivian was shivering next to her on the ground. Ida touched her forehead to see if she had a fever, but she wasn't sure. Something was definitely wrong. Feeling Ida's hand on her forehead, Vivian woke up.

"Hey, how are you feeling?" Ida stroked Vivian's clammy hair from her forehead.

"Not good." Vivian coughed and slowly dragged herself into an upright position. "I feel light-headed and my shoulder is throbbing."

"Well, we need to eat some real food today. That's probably why you feel light-headed." Ida offered hunger as an explanation but silently she worried that Vivian's wound had gotten infected. There was no way to know what might have been swimming in that river with them, given the runoff from two days of rain and all the debris they'd seen along the banks.

Vivian managed to get to her feet with Ida's help and braced herself against a large red oak. She tried to remember what they'd eaten last. A couple of apples yesterday? Blackberries the night before? Her foggy head couldn't recall. Had they walked one day or two since the river crossing? She was unsure.

"How long has it been since we crossed the river?" Vivian asked.

"Two days."

Vivian swiveled her body to mentally scale the height and position of the sun. It was still early. They shouldered their packs and began walking toward the sunrise. Her grandfather's map hadn't fared so well after heavy rain and a swim in the Chattahoochee. Its markings had blurred or disappeared entirely. The eastern edge of his route was damaged beyond recognition, so now Vivian was truly left to her own devices.

Vivian decided they should turn north in the hopes of crossing the road they'd previously followed. After a few hours of walking north, they stumbled out of a particularly thick patch of mountain laurel onto a wide footpath. It wasn't a road. There was no sign that wagons had traversed it, but the trail was well worn. If they were lucky, following the path to the east would lead them in the right direction.

As they stood in the opening around the path, Vivian could see a strange tall shape in the distance. It was tall and narrow, jutting skyward.

"What is that?" Vivian couldn't get her head around what she was seeing.

"I think it was part of an old building." Ida followed Vivian's gaze to the west. "Yeah, it looks like it might have been a few stories high."

From this distance, it looked like a finger-shaped green tower. But it was just a remnant of some tall building that was now covered in kudzu. Inland communities were the places that hadn't fared well in the exodus of the elite. With no coastal access and transportation at a standstill after fuel ran out, the dense southern forest that surrounded most land locked settlements had slowly swallowed up the structures that remained standing after the looting ended. Too bad, because if a village still existed here they'd have been able to find a doctor by now to see to Vivian's shoulder.

As the day progressed, Vivian began to feel worse. Even if she did find a rabbit or squirrel, her hands were shaking so badly that her bow would be useless. Her head swam and she swayed on her feet. Ida moved quickly to catch her.

Ida was afraid Vivian might fall at any moment, her gait was so unstable. They needed rest, food, and a healer. The best chance of finding all of those things was to get to Ida's family farm. They had to be getting close. She put her arm around Vivian's waist and insisted that Vivian lean against her. Ida felt Vivian's forehead. It was burning up. Worry enveloped Ida. If Vivian got too sick to walk, Ida knew she wouldn't be able to carry her.

The trail carried them northeast and Ida began to see landmarks that looked familiar. They were close. Eventually the path led into an open pasture. At the far edge of the open green, Ida saw a small gathering of exposed wooden structures. She recognized the old mill. They had made it. She helped Vivian stagger to the side of one of the buildings before Vivian stumbled and dropped to her knees. Ida couldn't get her back on her feet.

"I'm just going to rest here for a minute."

"Vivian, we're so close. Don't stop now." Ida tried to rouse Vivian, but the fever had claimed her and she was out cold. "Oh, Vivian, no. Wake up!"

Ida scanned the village from where she stood. She spotted Kent Riley just as he was about to climb up into the seat at the front of his buckboard.

"Kent! I need your help!"

Ida saw recognition slowly cross Kent's face. She was probably the last person he expected to see since she'd left the community more than a year ago. She no doubt also looked like a homeless urchin, starved and with several days of trail dirt, and now river sediment on her clothes. But Ida didn't care about those things at the moment. All that mattered was getting Vivian help.

CHAPTER TWENTY-SEVEN

K ent pulled the wagon up as close as he could to the porch so they'd have less distance to cover in case they had to carry Vivian. Ida climbed up into the wagon and helped Vivian sit up.

"Do you think you can walk?" Ida asked. Vivian nodded, barely opening her eyes.

The three front steps to the house were the toughest part of their journey. Ida was at just the right height to fit under Vivian's shoulder. Kent took position on the other side. Together, they all moved slowly toward the bedroom at the back of the house.

"Hang on to her for just a minute, Kent." Ida removed the white sheet sheltering the bed from dust.

Vivian collapsed onto the bed. Ida removed her boots and stood over her. Exhaustion was making it hard for her to focus.

"Kent, thank you for your help," Ida said finally.

"Are you sure you're okay, Ida?"

"I will be." Ida dusted at her soiled clothing. "I just need to get cleaned up and eat something. We ran into a bit of trouble a few days ago and Vivian was hurt."

"Well, what else can I do?"

"Would you mind terribly finding my brother? Samuel didn't know to expect me so he has no idea I'm here."

"I'll go find him." Kent pulled on his hat and headed for the door.

Alone, Ida could now see that Vivian's wound was not healing. How had she missed this earlier in the day?

Ida decided the first order of business was to get herself together before her brother arrived. She knew in her current state she would only worry him. Ida hurried to the bathroom, primed the dormant pump, and sloshed water into a pan near the claw-foot tub. No one had been living in the house since she'd left, but it was obvious that Samuel's wife, Rachel, had kept the place tidy in her absence. After Ida drank and splashed her face with water, she put on a rumpled blouse before rummaging the kitchen for food. Ida found just one jar of peaches. She ate half the jar, barely pausing to breathe between bites. Feeling a bit more human now, she placed some peaches in a bowl and carried them to Vivian.

"Sweetheart, can you eat something?" Ida brushed her palm across Vivian's forehead. Her face was hot to the touch.

Vivian's eyes fluttered. She responded with a hoarse voice. "Yes."

Ida held the bowl close as Vivian tried to rise up on the pillows. Ida was able to feed Vivian three small spoonfuls of peaches before Vivian sank down again, exhausted. It was at that moment that Ida heard quick footsteps in the house. Her brother's disheveled blond hair appeared in the doorway. He broke into a grin as she set the dish aside. She'd never been so happy to see anyone in her life.

"Ida!" Samuel hugged her tight. "You're back! I didn't know you were coming!" He held Ida away at arm's length to examine her. "Are you hurt? Are you okay? How did you get here?" And then he took notice of Vivian in the bed.

"Samuel, that's Vivian. She and I have been traveling together since I left Mississippi. I'm okay, but she's hurt. Can you get Francis?"

Samuel nodded. "Of course, right away. I'll stop by the house on my way and let Rachel know you're here. I'm sure she'll bring you both some food."

"Thank you. God, it's good to be home." Ida pulled him into another hug before he left to go in search of the local healer, Francis.

Now that help was on the way, Ida decided to remove Vivian's tattered jacket and shirt and attempt to clean her up a bit before Francis arrived. She found one of Samuel's shirts in a closet in the other room that she thought might fit well enough until she got them both some clean clothes. Ida refilled the basin with warm water and placed it on top of a small table by the bed with some clean towels. After another moment of consideration, Ida decided the best thing to do was to cut away Vivian's old clothing. She figured the garments were beyond repair. Ida fetched scissors and began to slowly cut at the jacket and thin cotton shirt underneath. Even in this injured condition, Ida was struck by how handsome Vivian was. Her breasts, now alert having been exposed to the cool air, were paler than her lean, tanned torso. Vivian was definitely thinner than when they'd first met, but still very attractive. Ida felt herself blush at the thought of their intimate moments together. What might have happened if Ida hadn't been with Vivian when she'd been struck by the arrow? Ida couldn't bear to think about it.

Ida soaked the soft cloth in warm water and cleaned Vivian's upper body. Vivian stirred as Ida softly caressed her chest, neck, and face with the warm, damp cloth, but she did not wake. Ida took special care cleaning around the wound in Vivian's right shoulder, which now looked angry and swollen. Vivian would definitely need the attention of the local healer as soon as possible. Even the burn over her left breast looked aggravated and red.

After doing the best she could with the cloth and water, Ida propped Vivian up enough so that she could slip her arms into Samuel's shirt. Vivian began to mumble.

"The river...can't make it..."

Ida gently laid Vivian back onto the pillow and covered her with a blanket, leaving the shirt loosely gathered but open in the front so Francis could more easily examine her shoulder.

"You're safe, sweetheart. We made it. Just rest," Ida whispered as she placed a soft kiss on Vivian's fevered forehead.

CHAPTER TWENTY-EIGHT

Not long after Ida had gotten Vivian cleaned and settled with a blanket, Samuel's wife, Rachel, showed up with a plate of food. It was nearly dusk when Samuel returned with the healer. He'd had some difficulty locating her.

Ida's niece, Cole, ran up as soon as the healer arrived by horseback.

"Who's sick?" asked Cole. She was barely six years old and hated to miss out on anything.

"A friend of Ida's," said Cole's mother, Rachel. "Say hello to your aunt Ida. She's been on a very long journey since we last saw her."

Cole gave Ida a tentative hug.

"Cole, how you've grown! I'm so pleased to see you." Ida knelt to be closer to her niece.

"Can I see your friend?" Cole asked.

"Not just yet. Let Francis have a look at her first." Rachel tousled Cole's hair before giving her a tight embrace.

"I hear you have a visitor who isn't well," said Francis. She dismounted and ambled toward the front steps carrying a small leather bag at her side. Her boots wore the miles that she traveled each week to see patients in need across North Georgia.

"She's in the spare room at the back of the house. This way. I'll show you."

Samuel and Rachel waited in the kitchen. Cole, her young mind having lost interest already, ran back outside. Francis pulled a chair close to Vivian's bedside as Ida stationed a lantern for optimum light. Francis rolled her shirtsleeves up and studied Vivian as if deciding where to begin her exam.

"Has she woken up since you laid her here?" asked Francis. She felt for a pulse and placed her broad, rough hand on Vivian's forehead.

"No. She said a few words when I put the clean shirt on, but she wasn't really awake. It was more like she was talking in her sleep." Ida hovered as Francis worked. "She was struck by an arrow in her right shoulder. That's the injury I'm most worried about, in addition to the fever."

Francis studied Vivian. She pulled back the blanket and lifted up the side of her shirt so that she could get a closer look at the wound on her shoulder.

"This looks infected. That could be the reason for the fever. Can you hold the lamp closer so I can take a look?" Francis reached into the leather satchel she'd carried in and retrieved a small set of tweezers. Ida held the lamp closer as Francis gently explored the wound. "I don't see foreign material in there, so that's good."

Francis opened the other side of the shirt and spotted the H-shaped burn. "What's this? Looks like a burn." She gently explored the old injury with the tips of her fingers. "This seems a tad inflamed too. But my best guess is that the shoulder is what's brought her condition to this point." She moved back to show Ida the opening in the skin. "See how this is red and puffy around the outside? That's likely the infection." She closed the shirt, pulled the blanket back up around Vivian, and sat back in her chair before turning to face Ida.

"She's probably not going to be well for several days. Are you sure you're able to tend to her?" Francis was never one to beat around the bush when a patient's needs were in question.

"Yes, I'll be able to take care of her. If you just tell me what needs doing, I'll do it."

"All right then." Francis stood and motioned for Ida to follow her out to the kitchen. "That shoulder is likely going to need some stitches, but it would be best to bring the infection down first. I can come back in a couple of days and see about sewing it up if she's lost the fever by then."

For the next twenty minutes, Francis measured out tinctures and teas with instructions to Ida about how each was to be administered. There was goldenseal tincture for the infection. Francis explained that this particular remedy wouldn't taste good so she'd have to mix it with something carrying a better flavor. Then there was turmeric and chamomile, diluted in water, to be applied directly to the wound. Lastly, boneset and catnip tea for the fever. Each herbal tonic was to be given three to four times a day until Ida saw a noticeable improvement. Francis vowed to come back before week's end to check Vivian's progress as she waved good-bye and pointed her mare toward the dirt roadway.

Rachel started toward their house to see about getting Cole bathed and ready for bed. Samuel lingered for a few minutes with Ida before joining his family.

"Are you sure you'll be okay here by yourself?"

"I'll be fine."

"Okay. Well, I'll check in with you tomorrow. Good night, Ida."

"Good night, brother. And thank you." Ida gave him a quick hug before he stepped off the porch and headed toward the flickering lights of his own home.

Ida watched Samuel disappear into the darkness before she returned to her parents' house, which now that she'd returned, was hers. Rachel had thankfully started a vegetable soup earlier in the evening. Vivian definitely needed to eat something more than few spoonfuls of peaches. Ida figured broth might be the most Vivian could handle tonight.

Ida set the steaming bowl aside while she braced Vivian's head a little higher on the pillows. Then, seated beside her on the bed, Ida slowly began to tempt Vivian's lips with the warm broth. Vivian opened her mouth just enough to allow the broth to settle on her tongue. Several spoonfuls later, Vivian began to stir.

Vivian fought to sit up, but her body conspired against her. Her arms felt heavy and uncoordinated, her whole being replete with aches.

"Just relax, we're safe."

The shape of Ida's head and torso were silhouetted by the golden hue of candlelight seeping into the darkened room from the open door behind her. Her quiet voice was soothing. Relishing Ida's tender caress, Vivian allowed herself to drift off into blackness.

CHAPTER TWENTY-NINE

Vivian blinked against the sunlight streaming across the bed. Where was she? She had dreamed last night that someone fed her soup. Was that real? She tried to focus; her eyes felt like they were filled with grit and fog. Her head hurt, her shoulder throbbed, and she still sensed a chill even though she saw that blankets were piled on top of her.

"Hello there."

Vivian heard a sweet, feminine voice. She was not alone. Ida's softly rounded figure greeted her sleepy gaze. Vivian smiled. She looked well and rested. Vivian was relieved.

"Hi." Vivian's voice cracked.

"Here, drink a little water." Ida held the glass to Vivian's lips.

"Thank you," said Vivian.

"I'm very happy to see you awake. You've been asleep since yesterday."

"I can't remember how we got here."

"We made it as far as the village just south of here. Luckily, my friend Kent was nearby with his wagon. He helped me get you home."

"I don't remember any of that." Vivian swallowed hard and blinked as if that would help her remember. "We're at your house?"

"Yes. We're home."

The fact that Ida had used the word "home" was not lost on Vivian. They were silent for a moment as Ida offered Vivian a cup with a bitter-tasting tea.

"The healer left me with some medicine for the infection and fever. This tea is part of it. I'm sorry. I know it doesn't taste very good."

Vivian couldn't take her eyes off Ida. Her face was bordered by feathery blond wisps that seemed to be attempting to escape the braided knot at the back of her head. Her pale fingers were delicate as they held the teacup up to meet Vivian's dry lips. Ida's blue-gray eyes, despite their cool color, had a softness that exuded warmth. Vivian had missed those eyes. She felt a knot form in her stomach as she reflected on what had happened to them at the river crossing. *What if something had happened to Ida?* Vivian wouldn't have survived such an event.

"Hey, these aren't my clothes." It was more of a statement than a question as Vivian realized that she was nearly nude under her shield of blankets.

"I'm afraid your shirt and jacket were ruined. I cut them off and helped you into one of my brother's shirts. Late last night you managed to get to the outhouse, with my assistance. But when you returned to bed you took your pants off."

"I have no memory of that either." Vivian blushed as she imagined a scene where she stripped down to her boxers.

"I'm not surprised. You had quite a high fever. You were more than a little out of it."

Vivian accepted some small bites of venison and potatoes from a plate that Ida offered. As she chewed, she considered her situation.

"Thank you, Ida." Vivian felt emotion rise in her throat, and it caused her to cough before she could continue. "I don't remember much about the past few days except that I wanted to keep you safe. I knew I wasn't able to do that in my injured state. I was so afraid. If anything had happened to you…"

Ida was surprised to see tears on Vivian's cheeks. She reached out to brush them away with her fingers. The tender gesture was meant to calm Vivian, but the contact also stirred her heart. She would never have known Vivian had been afraid. Vivian seemed to act without fear.

"Hey, we're okay now," Ida said. "You did keep us safe. If we hadn't jumped when we did I'm not sure we'd be here right now."

Vivian sniffed and wiped at the tears with the back of her hand. "Sorry, I don't know why I'm crying."

"Because you're hurt and tired. Why don't you rest a while and then we'll see about getting some more of this tea into your system." Ida set the cup aside. "Before I let you rest, though, I should put some of this medicine on your arm."

Ida soaked a cloth in a bowl of brownish liquid. She reached for Vivian's shirt but paused. "Okay?"

Vivian nodded.

Ida pulled Vivian's shirt away from her sore shoulder and gently placed the damp cloth over the wound. She repeated this several times, allowing the herb mixture from the cloth to seep into the open cut before closing the front of Vivian's shirt.

"Thanks," said Vivian.

"You just rest now." Ida placed her hand on Vivian's forehead for a moment as she stood. Vivian looked up at her through heavy lids and nodded. Ida knew it would only be a matter of minutes before Vivian was asleep again. She was weak and Ida guessed it would take at least another day of food and rest for her to regain some of her energy.

Ida removed the teacup and uneaten food, stepping quietly out of the room and into the kitchen. After tidying up a bit, she stepped back into the bedroom to find Vivian sound asleep. Ida settled herself into the chair at the bedside, allowing herself a few minutes to study Vivian in the warm morning light. Vivian's long dark lashes fluttered occasionally as she slept. Ida let her eyes take in the view of her defined forearm and long fingers. Ida couldn't help but admit how much she was falling for Vivian. She only hoped that after everything they'd been through together, Vivian had the same feelings for her. Ida had to fight the urge to curl up beside her. She knew that what Vivian needed was rest, and Ida wanted to do anything but rest when she was in bed with Vivian.

After lingering for a few more moments to study her, Ida stepped out of the room to begin her chores. She figured Samuel would be by soon to check on her. He wasn't the most trusting fellow, especially when it came to his younger sister housing a wayward outsider. Once he got a chance to know Vivian, Ida knew he'd feel differently.

❖

Late in the night, Ida was awakened by the muffled sounds of distress. She jolted awake, feeling disoriented for a few moments about where she was. Ida was sleeping in the spare room instead of with Vivian, and as the fog of sleep left her, she realized the sounds were coming from Vivian's room. She tossed the covers off and moved quickly down the hallway.

Vivian was tossing about as Ida drew near to the bedside. Ida tried to wake her.

"It's okay, you're okay! Vivian, you're safe."

"No, no, can't…have to leave…you don't own me!" Vivian fought against Ida, taking a swing at her and almost striking her in the face.

Ida decided she'd have to use her body weight to keep Vivian from tossing herself completely out of the bed. She climbed on top of Vivian, trying not to put pressure on her injured shoulder but still hold her arms down. "Vivian, wake up! It's me, Ida. Vivian, honey, can you hear me?"

"What?" Vivian's eyes fluttered open. The house was dark, but the moon shone brightly through the open curtains. "Where? Where am I? The river?"

Ida could tell from the heat coming off her body that Vivian was burning up. Worry seized her chest, making it hard for her to breathe for a minute.

"Ida?"

"Yes, Vivian, I'm here. You're safe."

Vivian slumped back on the sweat-dampened pillow. She was spent. Strands of moist hair clung to her forehead and her cheeks. She reached out and Ida captured her hand, pulling it to her face and kissing her palm.

"I'm here, sweetheart. Just lie still for a minute. I'm going to get you something to drink." Ida jumped off the bed and returned a moment later with a glass of water and a basin she'd also filled with water. She knew she needed to figure out a way to cool Vivian off a little. Maybe cold compresses would ease the fever's grip.

After she got Vivian to settle down enough to drink some water, Ida began to use cool compresses on her face and chest. She'd pulled the covers back and opened Vivian's shirt so that she could repeatedly place the cool rag on her skin.

Ida could tell Vivian was struggling against the fever to get her bearings. "I'm sorry. I didn't mean to wake you up."

"Don't worry about that, Vivian. Just try to relax. You need rest so that you'll feel better." Ida couldn't stop the tear that slowly rolled down her cheek. To have gone through everything they'd gone through and then have Vivian so weak and ill, it was more than Ida thought she could bear. In her mind she'd envisioned them coming home together, being with family, and enjoying getting to know each other. Getting Vivian this far and then losing her to a fever was not at all how Ida envisioned their future, and dammit, she wasn't going to let anything happen to Vivian. She sniffed and wiped at the tears with the back of her hand as she continued to dip the cloth in cool water and press it to Vivian's hot skin.

Ida wasn't sure how long she'd kept at the compresses, but eventually Vivian calmed and fell back asleep. When Ida felt her forehead, Vivian was still warm, but maybe her approach had helped ease her temperature a little. Vivian looked so weak that Ida couldn't bear to leave her alone. She curled up next to Vivian in bed.

She must have fallen asleep without realizing it. The next thing Ida knew, light was streaming in through the partially open window and she was spooning up against Vivian's back with her arm draped around Vivian's waist.

Ida sat up slowly and peered over Vivian's shoulder. She seemed to be sleeping peacefully. Ida touched her forehead. The fever had broken! *Thank God. Thank you, thank you, thank you.* Ida offered up prayers of gratitude.

Vivian began to stir. She rolled onto her back, right into Ida's arms. Her eyes fluttered open. "Ida?"

"Yes, baby, I'm here."

"You slept with me last night?"

"For a while. You had a rough spell for a few hours, but I think you're finally past the fever." Ida caressed Vivian's face. She was so incredibly relieved, hoping that they were now past the worst of things.

"I had bad dreams."

"I know. It's okay though. Everything is going to be okay now." Ida placed a tender kiss on Vivian's forehead as relief swept over her.

Chapter Thirty

Francis stopped by to check on Vivian's progress a couple days later. Ida noticed her approach by horseback from the kitchen window. She was drying her hands on a small towel when she welcomed Francis. After the usual pleasantries, Francis followed Ida into the house so that she could be officially introduced to Vivian. It was clear from Vivian's puzzled expression that she didn't remember meeting Francis.

"So, how's that shoulder feeling? Can I take a look?"

Vivian nodded.

Francis pulled up the sheet to give Vivian a buffer of privacy as she pulled back the right side of her shirt to expose the injured shoulder.

"Hmm." Francis leaned close. "I think this is gonna need a few stitches. Do you feel up to that?"

"I suppose, if you think that's best," said Vivian.

"This will likely hurt a bit. Why don't you sip a little of this laudanum for the pain?" Francis handed her a flask from her black leather bag.

Vivian nodded and took a couple of good swigs.

"Is there anything I can do to help?" asked Ida.

"I'm not sure you even want to see this. Have you ever seen anyone get stitched up before?"

"No, but I'd like to be helpful if I can."

"Okay, then. Why don't you sit on the other side of the bed

there and make sure Vivian doesn't squirm too much during these stitches?"

Ida settled on the bed next to Vivian and watched Francis thread the needle with dark strands of thread. She dunked the entire business into a small bowl filled with clear grain alcohol. Francis gave Vivian a confident smile. "Ready?"

Vivian nodded. As soon as the needle pierced the tender flesh, Ida could see Vivian's jaw clench. Vivian shut her eyes tightly against the visual of Francis repeatedly using the needle and thread. Ida reached for Vivian's free hand, and Vivian gratefully accepted it. Her grip was so strong, but Ida held firm, stroking Vivian's forearm as Francis made quick work of the dark sutures.

As Francis tied off the last stroke, Vivian finally exhaled against the pillows. Ida felt certain she would have been a blubbering basket case if she'd been the one to receive the stitches, but Vivian had been stoic through the entire event.

"You're lucky that Ida here has such a soft spot for hard luck cases." Francis smiled at Vivian as she stowed her things in her medical bag.

"I feel lucky."

"I'm the lucky one," said Ida.

At that, Francis smiled again at Vivian and gave her a wink. "Hmm, I see."

Ida blushed.

Francis patted Vivian's hand. "You're going to be fine, Vivian. You just need a few days of food and quality rest. Okay?"

Vivian nodded. She watched Ida and the healer exit the room and allowed her eyes to close. The stitches had hurt quite a bit, but now the pain in her right shoulder had subsided to a dull throb. After several minutes, she heard footsteps and opened her eyes expecting Ida but instead saw a youngster standing just inside the room.

"Hello," she said. "I'm Vivian."

"I'm Cole." The child moved a little closer to the bed but still kept a safe distance. "My first name is Ruth, and my middle name is Coleman, but everybody calls me Cole."

"My first name is Vivian, and my middle name is Wildfire, but everyone calls me Vivian."

"I like your name."

Cole moved a little closer. Her short dark hair was a rumpled mess, and her clothing was androgynous, so much so that had she not informed Vivian that her first name was Ruth she might have assumed the child was a boy. She smiled at the same mistaken gender identity that had also so often befallen her.

"Do you mind if I ask how old you are, Cole?"

"Six. How old are you?"

"Twenty-four."

"You're pretty old."

Vivian laughed and then coughed. Ida seemed to appear out of nowhere, offering her water.

"Cole, I said you could say hello, not pelt her with a bunch of questions," Ida chided her gently.

"I only asked a few questions."

"She's fine." Vivian sipped the water and smiled at Ida. "Really. Thank you for the water." Vivian pushed herself up to a seated position in the bed, causing Ida to regard her skeptically. "I think I'd like to try to walk around a little."

Even though Vivian still felt tired and weak, her restlessness was beginning to win out. Plus, she wasn't very good at having others tend to her needs.

Ida brushed her fingers affectionately through Cole's hair to smooth it down a bit. "Would you like to have lunch with us, Cole?"

"Yes." Cole smiled, not taking her eyes off Vivian.

Ida turned her attention to Vivian. "Maybe you should walk to the kitchen first, and then after you eat, Cole and I can show you around a little. But don't overdo things, okay?"

Vivian smiled and nodded as she slowly swung her legs over the edge of the bed. Just sitting up for a few minutes made her feel faint. She paused to let her blood pressure even out, then slowly eased her feet onto the floor. Ida reached to take her arm and Vivian didn't resist. She knew she wasn't entirely stable.

With slow movements, Vivian pulled on her trousers. They were freshly laundered thanks to Ida. But she still had Samuel's shirt, which was a bit oversized for her. After a few tentative steps, the three of them made their way to the small block table in the center of the kitchen. Vivian rolled up her sleeves as she settled into a chair, allowing her elbows to rest casually on the edge of the table.

"My mom always tells me not to put my elbows on the table," said Cole.

"Cole! Hush." Ida fussed at her from the stove nearby.

"Is your mom Rachel?" asked Vivian. "Your mom is right. I know better." She leaned back in her chair so that her arms fell away from the table and into her lap.

Vivian was still attempting to get her bearings on who all these new faces in her life were, and how exactly they were related to each other. She'd heard Ida and Rachel talk in hushed tones in the kitchen. She'd met both Rachel and Samuel, but only briefly.

"Rachel is my mom, Samuel is my dad, and Ida is my aunt. She and my dad are brother and sister." Cole seemed proud of herself for being able to explain all the connections.

Ida sat a plate of food in front of both of them then set one down for herself. Lunch was an array of vegetables: roasted potatoes and carrots with fresh tomatoes on the side. Vivian inhaled her plate deeply, realizing how hungry she was.

After lunch, Ida made quick work of the dishes and followed Cole and Vivian out to the porch. The weather was warm and clear, a perfect early autumn day. Vivian leaned with her good shoulder against the front porch railing as if that was something she did every day.

The truth was, while Ida was happy to see that Vivian was feeling better, she had enjoyed the intimacy of caring for her. While tending to Vivian, Ida was reminded of how lonely she'd been before they met. The last time she'd tended to someone who was ailing, it had been her mother. The days spent taking care of Vivian brought memories of that sad time with her mother, filling her with mixed emotions. Thoughts of her mother, whom she missed greatly, blended with thoughts of how she now considered Vivian part of her family. She was anxious for Vivian to be well enough for them to pick things up where they'd left off. She was missing Vivian's sensual touch. Ida blushed as she joined Vivian on the porch, as if Vivian were able to read her thoughts and knew where her mind had traveled.

"You're blushing. What were you just thinking?"

"Nothing." Ida gave her a sheepish sideways look as she allowed her fingers to entwine with Vivian's.

"It's probably the same thing I've been thinking."

"I hope so." Vivian raised Ida's fingers to her lips and kissed them. Ida felt that brief brush of Vivian's mouth all the way to her knees. "Would you like to walk around the place a little?"

"I would."

"Just know that if I see you getting the least bit fatigued, we're heading right back to the house."

"Yes, ma'am."

Cole ran ahead of them, stopping occasionally to pick up a stone to throw it or run a stick through the tops of the tall golden grass in the field that separated the two farmhouses. Ida explained that the house she occupied had belonged to her parents, who had passed away, and that Samuel and Rachel lived in the house that had belonged to her grandparents. The entire property encompassed about thirty acres, bordered on one side by a sizeable creek and a ground-fed spring on the other. A big old barn stood in between the two farmhouses, closer to Rachel and Samuel's place. Ida also explained to Vivian that their property sat at the foothills of the Blue Mountains.

Vivian stopped their stroll in its tracks and reviewed what Ida had said with wide eyes. "The Blue Mountains? We're close to them?"

"We're in them. You can see them from here. We can walk into the hills when you feel up to it."

Vivian looked around in wonder. She was indeed standing in a valley, surrounded on all sides by rolling blue ridges. She'd been here for days but hadn't been outside to get a better look at her environs. "I made it."

"We made it."

Vivian studied Ida's face. Was she finally living her destiny? Was Ida part of that destiny now?

"What?" Ida gave Vivian a puzzled look.

"Nothing."

Vivian took her eyes off Ida's lovely, upturned face for a moment to take in her surroundings. She'd actually made it to the Blue Mountains and she hadn't even realized it. But this was the place where she'd come to heal, in more ways than just one. It had to mean something that her body had begun the healing process here. Maybe her soul could find some recovery, too.

❖

Later that night, after Ida had gone to bed and the house was dark and silent, Vivian woke with a start. She sat on the edge of the bed for a moment, allowing her heart rate to slow. Another bad dream had pulled her from a restless sleep. She stood, pulled on trousers, and leaned against the door frame to steady herself before leaving the bedroom and walking out onto the long front porch.

Vivian didn't know what time it was, but the full moon had crested the mountain ridge that she could see from the porch railing. Now that she'd made it to the Blue Mountains, she was anxious to be out among them. To climb the high crests and look beyond. To get a view of the world around her.

She realized that over the past few days she'd been forced, through illness, to let her guard down with Ida. She'd needed Ida and she'd let Ida get close. She fought against the panic that rose in her chest at the thought that she not only wanted Ida, she'd needed her. Realizing that despite her best efforts to keep firm emotional boundaries in place, she hadn't. Maybe that was okay. Maybe that was the natural progression of things. Ida had given her no reason to believe she harbored anything close to resembling the cruelty that Elizabeth seemed to carry. She had known Ida to be beautiful, inside and out.

She also knew that she wanted Ida. Ever since the night they'd made love she'd longed to be with Ida again, but she knew that would further weaken any barriers she'd tried to keep in place between them. Ida had a way of climbing over the fortifications she'd set in place like they were a child's play set. Once Ida truly got inside her heart, she'd be done for. There'd be no saving herself then. She already suspected that she was falling for Ida, and the longer she lingered here, the harder it would be not to. Would that be the worst thing? Not for her, but maybe for Ida. In the deepest part of her heart Vivian truly believed that Ida deserved better. What did she bring to a union such as this? Nothing.

She was lost in her downwardly spiraling thoughts and didn't realize Ida had approached until she felt a gentle touch on her arm.

"Are you okay?" Ida looked up at her as she covered a yawn with her hand.

"I'm fine. You didn't need to check on me."

"I was thirsty, so when I went to get water I looked to see how you were doing." Ida hugged herself and took a deep breath. "It smells so good here, doesn't it?"

"Yes, it does."

They were quiet for a few moments. Vivian wanted to say something to Ida, but she wasn't sure how to begin.

"Ida…"

Ida was standing very near and looked in Vivian's direction. The moonlight was reflected in her eyes. The look on her face seemed pensive and it caused Vivian to falter, but she forced herself to continue.

"Ida, I want to thank you for everything you've done for me. I want you to know I'm grateful."

Ida felt her stomach sink as she watched Vivian struggle with her words. She knew there was a "but" coming. She tried to brace herself for whatever Vivian was about to say.

"Have you thought about what happened at Rebecca's farm?"

Ida wasn't sure if she was talking about the night they'd made love, or the fight that had followed, or the men who'd attacked them.

"I have. A lot happened while we were there."

"I worry that I'm not the person you think I am, Ida." Vivian shoved her hands in her pockets and looked down at the floorboards. "I've done things."

"We've all done things, Vivian."

"I'm pretty sure I've done things that you would never do and you'd probably think less of me if you knew about them."

"Are you talking about the men you killed? You had no choice, Vivian."

"Other things, too."

"Why are you telling me this now?" They'd walked together for weeks. Why was Vivian just now wanting to reveal some flaw she perceived in her character?

Vivian looked over at Ida with a pained look on her face. "I worry that you're expecting us to be together in a way that I can't be."

"What does that mean?" Ida felt herself chill despite the warm evening and hugged herself more tightly.

"I'm not good enough for you, Ida. I know I'm not." Vivian's voice broke.

"Vivian, don't say that." Ida had started to cry, which was the last thing she wanted to do. "Please don't quit on us before you even give us a chance. You're just tired and you need to rest."

Vivian sniffed and brushed away a tear with the back of her hand. Ida wanted to reach out to her but she was unsure if she should. Vivian seemed to be struggling with something bigger than just their relationship. Or maybe she was misreading things.

Vivian looked at Ida, the moonlight highlighting the path of tears on her cheeks. "I don't think I'll be any good at this. I…I don't know how to let you get close and keep you there."

"You don't have to know everything right now. Just give it some time. Give us time to know each other better. The closeness will come by itself if it's meant to." Ida could stand the space between them no longer, so she put her hands on Vivian's arms, turning her so that they faced each other fully. "Promise me you'll just give us a little more time?"

Vivian nodded but didn't seem convinced of what Ida was saying.

"Vivian, if you decide you don't want to be here then I certainly won't put pressure on you to stay. This has to be good for both of us or it won't work for either of us."

Vivian nodded again and a tear slowly trailed down her cheek.

"You're a good person, Vivian. I know it. I've seen who you really are." Ida leaned into Vivian, pressing her cheek against Vivian's chest. "I'm as scared as you are about the way I feel. But let's not let fear stop us from trying, okay?"

She pulled Vivian more tightly against her and they held each other for some time before turning and going back into the dark house.

CHAPTER THIRTY-ONE

More than a week had passed since Ida's return, and today was the day she and Rachel had planned to do some canning. Ida carried the crate of glass jars in both hands and kicked the door shut behind her as she entered the kitchen, where Rachel was starting the process.

"Hey, there. I started cooking the apples. We almost let them get too ripe," said Rachel. She was busy at the wood stove, stirring a huge pot.

Ida set the jars on the far end of the table. Rachel was wearing one of Samuel's old shirts over hers, no doubt to guard against splatters. Her dark brown hair, the same color as Cole's, was pulled back into a ponytail away from her face. Her brown eyes were dancing. Ida enjoyed canning, but didn't have the same glee that Rachel seemed to have about it. Cooking something that wouldn't be savored until later was too much delayed gratification for Ida. She enjoyed much more the act of cooking and then eating right away, especially baked goods, like pies. Ida's face must still have carried the small frown she'd brought over from her house. Rachel noticed right away.

"What's wrong?"

"Nothing's wrong," said Ida.

"Tell me. Isn't that half the fun of canning? That we stand around solving all the world's problems while we're doing it?"

"I suppose."

"So? What's the matter? Did you and Vivian have a fight?"

"Why would you assume this has anything to do with Vivian?" Rachel gave Ida an *Are you kidding me?* sideways look.

"We didn't have a fight. We just had a talk the other night and now I can't help…worrying."

"Worrying about what?"

"That she doesn't feel the same way I do."

"You can't be serious," said Rachel with amusement in her voice.

"What do you mean by that?"

"Seriously?"

"Yes, seriously."

"Ida, sweetheart, Vivian never takes her eyes off you. And you're no more subtle than she is, except apparently to each other." Rachel chuckled softly as she stirred the large steaming pot.

Ida stood with her hands on her hips across the kitchen. "What are you saying?"

"I'm saying that it's clear to me, and to Samuel, that the two of you are completely in love with each other. It's written all over Vivian's face every time she looks at you."

"Then what is she so afraid of?"

"She's afraid? Is that what she said?"

"Well, sort of." Ida studied her hands resting on the table. "That and I think she also believes she's not good enough for me. She's said as much."

"You two have slept together, right?" Rachel began to spoon some of the apples into glass jars.

Ida's face turned scarlet. She glanced away from Rachel and out the window, biting her lower lip. The minute Rachel mentioned sex, Ida felt her insides flip.

Rachel moved to stand near Ida and gently put her hands around her shoulders. "I'm sorry, that was too personal. I didn't mean to upset you, Ida."

Ida turned to look at her just as a tear spilled over and down her cheek.

"Oh, sweetie, it can't be that bad. Come here and sit down. I'll fix us some tea." Rachel pulled Ida toward a chair. Ida slumped in, propped her elbows on top of the table, and rested her chin in her hands.

"It is that bad," said Ida.

"Talk to me." Rachel filled the kettle and nestled it near the large pot before taking the chair nearest Ida.

"I've completely fallen for her and I have no idea how she really feels. I have no idea if she's going to wake up tomorrow and tell me she's leaving. In which case, I would be devastated. I feel like I have no control over what's happening between us because I have no idea what's really going on in her head." Ida sniffed and looked over at Rachel.

"Well, what are you going to do about it?"

"I don't know." Ida felt completely frustrated.

The whistle on the teakettle began to squeal. As Rachel got up to fill their cups, she turned to Ida. "I have an idea."

"I'd love to hear it." Ida accepted a steaming cup from Rachel as she returned to her seat at the table.

"Well, I think part of the complication with you two is that up to this point, your relationship has been on uneven terms. Vivian was quite ill when she first arrived so that put you in a position of being her caregiver. Not only that, but she's in your home, with your family. She's completely in your world. Now, I could be entirely wrong about this, but I get the feeling that Vivian is a strong person and needing someone's help like that was probably really hard for her. I would hazard to say that she's probably not feeling so good about herself right now."

"I never thought of it that way," said Ida.

"So, I think if we can get you two interacting in a more equal way, then nature will take its course."

"Vivian did say this morning that she wants to work around the farm. I think *contribute* was the word she used."

"I knew it," said Rachel triumphantly.

"Excuse me, but since when did you get so smart?" Ida raised an eyebrow in Rachel's direction as she sipped her tea.

"How do you think I got your brother to propose?"

"I guess I assumed it was all his doing."

"That's because that's what he was led to believe," said Rachel.

"I guess I came to the right person for advice then."

"Ida, you just be your usual enchanting self and everything else is going to take care of itself. I promise."

Rachel beamed with excitement.

"Wait, what else are you thinking?"

"Let's have a double date. I'll make dinner." Rachel nonchalantly sipped her tea. "What are you doing tomorrow night?"

"I think I have a double date." Ida smiled, feeling relieved and hopeful.

CHAPTER THIRTY-TWO

Vivian checked her reflection in the mirror. Rachel had extended an invitation for Vivian and Ida to join them for dinner, and she wanted to look her best. She tucked her shirttail into her belted trousers and ran her fingers through her hair once more.

After working with Samuel in the field for the day, she'd gotten to learn the layout of the farm. Vivian had also discovered that he'd had a problem with rabbits getting into what was left of their vegetable plot. Vivian offered to cull that brood for Samuel a bit with her bow. A few of the rabbits she'd killed would be their dinner this evening. Vivian was more than happy to be able to subsidize in some way for her food and shelter.

After Samuel realized how gifted Vivian was with a bow, he made plans for them to hunt for deer. Vivian had readily agreed. The weather was cooling off considerably, so it would be the perfect time to cure the meat. As a matter of fact, Vivian was realizing as she stepped out now onto the front stoop that she needed her coat. She quickly retrieved it and waited for Ida so that they could walk to Rachel and Samuel's place together. She was struck by the thought that hunting with Samuel and curing meat for winter sounded an awful lot like planning for the future. It was true that she was feeling better about things. Ever since the night she and Ida had talked, her fears had subsided a little.

After a few moments, Ida joined her on the porch. Vivian

smiled rather sheepishly as she offered her arm to Ida. It was quickly accepted. Vivian felt light as a feather. This was shaping up to be a good evening.

Ida stepped through the doorway first when they arrived, and Samuel helped her out of her coat. She couldn't help but notice her brother's clean-shaven face and pressed shirt. She knew that Rachel had probably coached him about everything before they arrived. Ida appreciated her big brother's warm welcome after what she figured had been a hard day of fieldwork. Vivian had mentioned on the walk over that earlier in the day she'd been helping Samuel cut and store hay in the barn. However, since she wasn't quite back to full strength, Vivian's workday had to be shorter than Samuel's.

Samuel took Vivian's coat next, and the four of them chatted genially while Rachel finished setting bowls of rabbit stew along with a bowl of hot apples from the canning they'd done the previous day on the table. Samuel disappeared for a bit before returning with a pint jar of blackberry wine.

Ida felt almost giddy. So far, the evening was going beautifully. Rachel's idea for a double date was perfect, and Vivian looked gorgeous and had been completely attentive. Just the thought of that made Ida's heart do little butterfly flips in her chest. Ida had abandoned her usual workday slacks for a dress, and Vivian had been sweet enough to comment on how pretty she looked. Ida's hair was pulled into a knot at the back of her head, but a soft curl of blond hair had blown out along the way. When she caught Vivian looking at her, she blushed and self-consciously tucked the errant lock behind her ear.

Ida looked over to admire Vivian. Vivian had put on a clean white shirt that framed her dark, strong features. Her black hair hung loosely near her jawline. Ida found the whole package incredibly sexy. Vivian smelled of rose soap on the walk over, and all Ida could think about was snuggling into the crook of Vivian's neck and kissing her. *Over and over and over.* Ida realized that Rachel had been talking to her and she snapped her attention back to the present.

"I'm sorry, what?"

Samuel covered his smile with his hand.

"I said, we're ready if everyone would like to sit."

"Thank you so much, Rachel. The food looks amazing." Vivian pulled a chair out for Ida before she sat down.

Samuel gave Rachel a knowing look. Ida saw the exchange, but luckily, Vivian had been distracted getting Ida settled. Ida was going to have to do something especially nice for Rachel in return for this dinner.

Everyone held hands while Samuel said grace. Ida couldn't help but notice that Vivian seemed reluctant to release her hand following the mealtime prayer. She could have sworn that Vivian even squeezed her fingers slightly before she dropped her hand to her lap.

Dinner was a huge success. Rachel was an amazing cook and the conversation was light and at times even jovial. It seemed that the energy of attraction between Ida and Vivian had infected everyone. Ida noticed how sweet Rachel and Samuel were being to each other throughout dinner, flirting as if they hadn't already been married for seven years. They told funny stories of their early years together and charming stories about being new parents after Cole's birth. Cole was spending the night at a friend's house to give them all some "adult time."

As the evening progressed, and the blackberry wine had rounded the table more than once, Ida was sure she could see some of the tension Vivian had been carrying leave her shoulders. It was such a treat to hear Vivian genuinely laugh. God, she was so gorgeous in all the right ways. Ida began to feel that insatiable ache building in her core. As much as she was enjoying dinner, she couldn't wait to get Vivian alone.

The plan she and Rachel had settled on had been to have dinner, and then as a group play a game of cards or some other party-type activity. But now, all Ida could think about was getting Vivian to herself. She decided during dessert that if the suggestion of games came up she was going to propose a different direction. Vivian had been so attentive to her all night that Ida felt her confidence rise along with her body temperature.

Vivian left the room to help Samuel bring in some wood for a fire, which gave Ida a moment to help Rachel alone in the kitchen.

"Ida, you're glowing."

"I feel like I'm glowing," Ida was practically giddy with excitement. "Rachel, I can't thank you enough for this. I think this was just what we needed."

"Do you still want to try your hand at cards?" asked Rachel.

"I had something else in mind. But suggest a game so that I can suggest my alternative plan."

"Consider it done."

They joined Vivian and Samuel back in the living room.

"Hey, should we play a game or something? It's still early, and I don't think I've had too much wine to not be useful as a card partner." Rachel moved to stand next to Samuel by the fire, who then lovingly wrapped his arms around her slender waist.

"That was such an amazing dinner, Rachel," said Ida. "I was wondering if Vivian would like to take a walk. It's such a beautiful evening. And that way you two could enjoy some time to yourselves, which we all know is a rare event."

Ida looked in Vivian's direction to assess her level of interest in that suggestion. Vivian was thankfully smiling broadly.

"I'd love to go for a walk," said Vivian.

After they said their good-byes, with promises to make dinner together a more regular event, Vivian and Ida struck out on their evening stroll. The air was crisp but not so sharp as to be considered cold. The night sky was clear and the stars blinked knowingly overhead. The moon was half full so they didn't really need a lantern for their promenade. After they were several yards from the house, Vivian offered her arm for Ida, who gladly accepted.

"That was fun," said Vivian.

"It really was. Rachel and Samuel are a joy to be around. I feel lucky to have them both in my life. And Cole, too, for that matter."

"Yeah, Cole is a great kid. I told her today I'd teach her to shoot with a bow."

"I hope she's better at it than I was."

"In your defense, I think you were distracted."

"Blissfully so," said Ida. "You do realize that Cole adores you."

"I'm not sure about that," said Vivian shyly.

"I am. And she might not be the only one."

"Hmm, is that so?" Vivian was happy it was dark out because Ida couldn't notice the color she felt sure was rising to her face. Throughout the entire evening, every time Ida had touched her, no matter how fleeting, the spot where they'd connected left heat. Vivian tried her best to keep her thoughts in check, but frequently during dinner she found herself staring at Ida's lips. Then her mind would wander with thoughts of where she'd like to direct those lips. And for that matter, where she'd like to place her lips on Ida.

They'd been walking for a while but at a very slow pace. After almost a half hour, they'd only now made it as far as the pond just past the boundary of the George property. The moon seemed unusually bright as it cast its reflection on the smooth surface of the undisturbed water. Vivian couldn't resist tossing a small stone just to see the moonlight bounce in ripples across the surface. She heard Ida speaking softly about something, but Vivian couldn't focus on the words. Ida's lips mesmerized her. Ida's words were cut short by Vivian's mouth on hers. She could no longer ignore the excruciating impulse she felt to kiss Ida.

Relaxing against Vivian, Ida slowly moved her hands up Vivian's arms, then encircled Vivian's neck and drifted through Vivian's thick dark hair along the way. Ida felt Vivian tease her lips with her tongue until Ida relented and opened to her. The kiss was soft and then hard, all the while sensuous. Ida felt her stomach sink and her knees go weak. And then that ache again deep, deep inside. What was Vivian doing to her? Her body was no longer under her control. If Vivian kept kissing her like this, Vivian could ask anything of her and she would be unable to refuse.

Ida pressed into Vivian as she grabbed the back of Ida's coat to pull them closer together. She could feel Vivian's pelvis move against hers. Suddenly, Ida couldn't breathe and broke their kiss.

Vivian took Ida's face in her hands and tilted her head up so that she could study her face in the moonlight.

"Ida, I know I'm not very good at telling you how I feel."

Vivian placed a kiss on Ida's forehead and pulled her head to her chest. "You make me feel things that I've never felt before." Vivian wrapped Ida in her strong arms.

Not since Elizabeth had Vivian wanted to kiss someone so badly, and even that kiss had felt nothing like the kisses she'd shared with Ida. Every time she was with Elizabeth, she sensed that Elizabeth held back. That she calculated their every encounter, doling out intimacy in small doses. Vivian knew it now, even though at the time she chose to ignore it. What she felt from Ida was very different. What she felt from Ida felt right.

CHAPTER THIRTY-THREE

Vivian shifted in bed, folding her arm behind her head so that she could roll onto her side facing Ida. Hours had turned into days. Days had turned into weeks. Vivian had now been a resident of the George property for three weeks and she was feeling almost back to her old self. Her torn shoulder had healed well, and the muscle was coming back in her upper arm. In this time span she had grown even more attached to Ida, who was pressed against her in bed. She savored the sleepy early morning time when Ida slept so soundly next to her. She could stare at her lovely face without discovery. Ida's features were completely relaxed, her golden tufts spread across her pillow.

Maybe this was how love happened, gradually, slowly eclipsing everything else in your world until all you could see was the person who'd captured your heart. Sometime between their late night talk on the porch and this moment, Vivian had begun to relax. The fear she'd felt hovering above her like a small dark cloud had lifted, at least for now.

The ever-brightening sunrise began to bathe the room in a warm glow. As streaks of light crisscrossed the bed, Ida began to stir. She smiled when she saw that Vivian was already awake and watching her.

Vivian caressed Ida's arm, exposed above the covers. "Good morning."

"Good morning to you." Ida covered her face as she yawned. "How is it you always wake up before me?"

"Just lucky, I guess." In truth, Vivian usually woke with a jolt as if coming out of some tense dream. She would then remember where she was and her nervous system would settle. She wondered if she'd ever fully settle down and be able to sleep as soundly as Ida.

Vivian positioned herself so that her mouth was next to Ida's. She delivered a kiss that was tender and sweet, one that only Ida deserved. As they kissed, Vivian ran her fingers through Ida's hair. Despite Vivian's best efforts, she began to arch her body into Ida's as she couldn't help noticing how good Ida's body felt pressed against hers. She felt wetness gathering between her legs, coupled with a deep ache for Ida to touch her. All the while, their mouths explored each other. Ida's lips had drifted to the left so she could sprinkle light kisses down Vivian's jawline to her neck, sending chills down Vivian's arms. Vivian wanted to give Ida a chance to ease into her morning, but she was having a very hard time keeping her hands from roaming the soft curves of Ida's body now pressed so tightly against hers.

"I know you just woke up, but I want you...now."

"You can have me."

Vivian felt Ida's fingers at the bottom edge of her shirttail as Ida trailed her fingertips across Vivian's stomach. Ida pushed the material of the shirt up in an attempt to get Vivian to take it off. After uttering a small moan at Ida's hand on her midsection, Vivian obliged and pulled the loose cotton shirt off over her head. Now with even less of a barrier between them, Vivian could see Ida's nipples harden with desire through the sheer fabric of her nightgown.

"I love the way you kiss me." Ida ran her hands through Vivian's hair, placing a kiss on top of her forehead.

"Ida, please forgive me."

"Forgive you for what?" Ida shifted next to Vivian so that she could see her face.

"For being afraid to let you into my heart," said Vivian. "I say that, but the truth is you are in my heart. I could no more deny you entry than I could go without water or air."

Ida caressed her face and let her fingers gently trail across Vivian's shoulders. "I've fallen for you. I've fallen so hard, Vivian." She needed to say those words to Vivian, regardless of how Vivian responded. Not saying them didn't make them any less true.

"I had made a vow to myself that I wouldn't let anyone close." Vivian traced her forefinger along the edge of Ida's face as she searched for words. "Not so much physically close, but emotionally close. When I look at you like this, so close, so unguarded, I feel something. I feel it deep in my chest." Vivian wrapped her arms around Ida and held her tight, resting her cheek on the top of Ida's head as she spoke. "I need you and that scares me."

"Vivian, every relationship involves risk." Ida stroked Vivian's back as she spoke. Ida pulled away a little so that she could see Vivian's face. She wanted so much to heal Vivian's hurt. Ida knew that opening up to Vivian held risk for her, too. But feeling the intensity of emotion between them was overriding any sense of caution.

Ida pulled Vivian's head down until their lips met. She kissed Vivian for some time, until she could no longer stand the want pounding in her chest.

"Vivian, I won't hurt you."

"You don't know that. You can't know that."

"I promise to try."

Vivian was at a loss for what to say. Several things rolled around in her head, mutating into a jumbled mess of fear and rationalizations. Until finally, recognition of the truth rose to the surface. She knew that she was in love with Ida. Deeply. Desperately. Acknowledging that truth to herself seemed to loosen some tether inside Vivian. Tears began to gather at the edge of her lashes. Vivian buried her face in Ida's hair.

Ida cradled Vivian's head in her arms, holding her tightly. She kissed Vivian's cheek and whispered against her ear, "Please trust me. Don't be afraid to let me in."

Vivian looked at Ida, the wet paths on her face glimmering in the early morning sunlight. She allowed Ida to pull her into a deep kiss. One that was warm and salty from her tears.

Vivian regarded Ida with affection. The soft swell of her breasts, the slight curve of her stomach, and the pleasing contour of her shapely hips.

"Ida, you are so beautiful."

Vivian swept her fingertips lightly along the outside of Ida's breasts, following the rounded contours down to her hips, where she began to gently push down her underwear. Vivian followed the downward movement of the garment, trailing kisses all along Ida's thighs.

Vivian was trying to read every subtle signal that Ida was sending with her fingers and her lips as she explored the ample landscape of Ida's form as if it were the topography of some sacred place. Vivian watched Ida's face closely as they moved against each other in a sensual dance. They climaxed simultaneously with such force that Vivian felt as if something broke loose inside her. All that she'd been holding back broke free—the anger, distrust, desire for some cosmic revenge. It all came undone. Her heart pounded loudly in her ears. She sensed her flight response. It was as if she were standing on the edge of an abyss about to tumble into the blackness below. Her breathing was shallow, her eyes wild and unfocused.

"It's okay, Vivian. Let go. I've got you. You're safe. It's okay to let go." Ida tenderly kissed Vivian's temple and held her tight.

Eventually, Vivian's frantic breathing subsided. Ida held her close as she felt her body finally relax next to hers.

"I've got you."

Chapter Thirty-four

Vivian pulled her jacket closed and buttoned it as she stepped off the porch. It was a chilly morning. Her breath puffed in front of her and then vanished, swallowed up by a light wind. Ida was planning to do some baking this morning. Vivian knew she needed to get out of the house or she'd either keep trying to distract Ida from her task or she'd want to eat everything Ida was cooking. Neither course of action was particularly helpful. Besides, a walk up to the ridge would do her good. Since her recovery, Vivian found herself wanting to take more walks up into the foothills of the Blue Mountains. Ida had been right when she'd said there was something special about this place. Vivian felt it, too. There was a peace that settled over Vivian's spirit when she crested the ridge and looked out over the blue ridges.

As she cut across the yard, the dead brown grass crackled under her boots. It almost sounded as if there might be a bit of frost pushing up from the ground. Vivian turned the collar of her jacket up around her ears. It would be chilly for another hour or two until the sun got a little higher in the sky. She stepped onto the dirt road in front of Ida's place and headed north toward an overlook she'd discovered on one of her recent hikes.

Quick footsteps approached and Vivian turned to see Cole running in her direction from the neighboring house.

"Hey, Vivian! Where are you going?"

"Just taking a walk up to the ridge."

"Can I come?"

"It's okay with me, but go tell your mom where you'll be. I'll wait here for you." Vivian smiled as she watched Cole sprint back toward the house from the road. "And put on a jacket!" Vivian yelled after her.

Cole returned in a matter of minutes and they began following a trail that left the roadway and headed up toward the ridge that overlooked the valley. They walked silently except for the sound of dry leaves crunching under each footfall. Sweet gum, red oak, poplar, and maple trees surrounded them and had begun changing into their fall colors and dropping dead leaves onto the forest floor.

Halfway up the ridge Cole found something that caught her attention. An old snakeskin was wedged between two saplings growing close together at their bases. Using a stick, Cole picked up the long and narrow translucent skin.

"That was a big one." Vivian leaned closer but couldn't really make out what sort of snake had worn the skin. It could have been a copperhead. They seemed the most prevalent here. The skin had likely been shed near the end of summer so it'd been on the ground for some time.

"Why do they shed their skin?" asked Cole. She held the skin close to her face to study it.

"They outgrow it. Kind of like when you have to get new clothes because your old ones get too small for you."

"How can they outgrow their skin? We don't outgrow ours." Cole looked up at Vivian with a puzzled expression on her face. Her eyebrows were scrunched slightly as if she wasn't quite sure she accepted the explanation.

"Snakes are different from us. They move without legs, too. I think that might be even stranger than shedding skin."

"Can I keep this?" Cole was still holding the thin skin with the stick.

"If you want to. Hang it on that branch and we'll get it when we walk back down to the house."

Cole did as Vivian suggested, and they resumed their gradual climb up the trail. The crest of the ridge could be seen through the trees not too far ahead of them.

"My grandfather used to say that the snake is a symbol of life. A symbol of throwing off the old and continuing to live."

"Throwing off the old what?" Cole asked. She was walking behind Vivian, whacking trees with a stick as they passed by. Vivian thought that it was a good thing they weren't trying to hunt. This had not been the quietest walk she'd been on.

"Throwing off whatever holds us back from growing, not just physically growing but spiritually growing." Vivian stopped and turned to face Cole on the trail. "Maybe you need to move to a different place, or maybe you start a family, or maybe you fall in love...or maybe you are afraid of something and that fear is holding you back."

"Oh, I get it."

Vivian smiled. Cole was a terrific kid, genuinely curious and sincere. Vivian had never spent much time with children, but she was growing very fond of Cole. She realized that she didn't really talk to Cole as some people might speak to a child. Vivian talked with her as if she were maybe capable of understanding more.

As they crested the ridge, they stepped out onto a large granite outcropping that was free of trees. The small clearing around the large stone surface afforded a view of the blue ridges spread out before them. Although today they weren't only blue. They were blue mixed with yellows and reds as the hardwoods signaled the arrival of autumn. Fall had arrived and the color flamed across the ridges.

They settled down on the rock to enjoy the vista before them. The early morning sky was clear so that the moon was still barely visible against the blue. More of her grandfather's words came to her as she sat looking up at the partial moon. *The snake sheds its skin the way the moon sheds its shadow.*

After sitting for a little while, Vivian and Cole turned back and began walking down the mountain toward the farm.

CHAPTER THIRTY-FIVE

Ida fussed with her hair in the mirror as she put the finishing touches on her Sunday best. The Sabbath had arrived at the end of a very pleasant week. Ever since their dinner at Rachel and Samuel's house, things had seemed back on track for Vivian and Ida. They continued to break through whatever emotional barriers existed between them, growing closer with each passing day. Ida had never felt so happy.

Ida stepped out of the bathroom to find Vivian sitting quietly at the table waiting for her. This would be the first time that Ida had attended church since they'd returned. She felt like it was finally time for Vivian to have her introduction to the larger community. The best way to achieve that was Sunday service.

More than a century ago, churches had almost completely disappeared. Not because people ceased to have faith as much as they ceased to have faith in something larger than themselves. Society over the preceding decades had become more and more secular. And as populations focused on *self* more than *other* or community, the need for the fellowship of the church faded into history. When the collapse happened, communal gatherings mattered again.

Ida wasn't sure she would describe herself as particularly religious, but she would never doubt the strength of kinship and support that her local church group offered. It was one of the things she'd missed when she was down south with Kate. She wanted Vivian to experience the communal gathering firsthand, now that she was becoming a part of the community herself.

They rode together on the narrow front seat of the buggy. Ida had allowed Vivian to handle the reins. Ida snuggled close against the early morning chill. Several horses and buggies were already tied to hitching posts near the small white wood-sided building by the time they arrived. Members of the congregation were speaking in friendly voices to each other and settling into long wooden pews when Vivian and Ida entered the sanctuary. Vivian pulled off her hat and Ida took her free hand, pulling her to a seat about halfway up the aisle.

Bringing Vivian to the service was like making a public declaration that they were a couple. Ida hoped Vivian didn't sense her nervousness. It wasn't that she had any doubts about how she was feeling about their relationship, but it was always stressful to invite potential comments from others. She smiled when she saw Rachel, Samuel, and Cole pass through the entry and head in their direction. Ida had picked an open pew in the hopes that they would arrive and settle in next to Vivian, which they did. Now Ida had the visual support of her brother, which meant a lot.

A few friends came over to introduce themselves. James said hello to Samuel and gave Ida a big hug before introducing himself to Vivian. James had a son, Marc, who was one of Cole's closest friends. Marc wasn't feeling well, so he and his mother had stayed home.

Next came Ben. His daughter, Jessica, stood shyly in front of him as he reached out his hand in greeting to Vivian. Ida fussed over Jessica, commenting on how much she'd grown. Jessica was only slightly younger than Cole and completely adorable in her dress with the tiny floral print fabric.

Ida was happy to discover that Chris, the woman she'd been involved with for more than a year before she left for south Mississippi, was not in attendance. Ida wasn't looking forward to their first meeting, and she certainly didn't want to add any tension to Vivian's first public appearance.

Piano music began, signaling for everyone to settle into seats. A man in a dark suit moved to stand behind the podium. Opening a tattered book that rested on the stand next to him, the man began to speak in a strong, but soothing voice. "Today I will read from Colossians chapter two, verse eight." He looked down at the text in the book as he read. "See to it that no one takes you captive by philosophy and empty deceit, according to human tradition…"

He closed the book and smiled at those seated in front of him. "In the olden days, we turned toward philosophy and science and away from God. We allowed ourselves to be surrounded by those who doubt the power of unseen forces at work in our daily lives. Forces like doubt, fear, anxiety, mistrust, and greed. I'd like to talk today about how God appointed gratitude and love as guardians for our souls against these forces."

Ida enjoyed the sermon. The minister was calling on the congregation to support each other with gratitude and love. So that, knit together, they would provide a safe haven for each other against the harsh demands of surviving in the world. And in doing so, would not just survive, but actually live with abundance. He may have intended other messages as well, but this was the part that captured Ida's attention. And she did feel grateful for many things in her life, not the least of which was the woman seated next to her, listening intently to the words spoken from the front of the sanctuary.

As he drew his message to a close, he signaled for all to stand for the closing hymn, "In the Garden."

Ida's voice faltered as emotion knotted in her throat. This hymn had been one of her mother's favorites, and she was unable to hear the tune without conjuring her mother's sweet face. As she attempted to wipe at her tears with the back of her hand, Samuel reached over to offer his handkerchief. She smiled and accepted, sniffing and dabbing at her eyes. Ida felt Vivian put a comforting arm around her shoulder as she joined in the chorus.

By the time the song ended, Ida had gathered herself enough that she could chat easily with other folks as they departed the sanctuary. She introduced Vivian to numerous local residents. There would be no way Vivian could possibly remember them all, but that would come with time. Vivian met each introduction with an open and friendly manner. She seemed truly at ease amongst Ida's friends.

The oddest part of all of this was that Kate wasn't there. The person who'd been closest to Ida wasn't there to meet the woman she was falling madly in love with. Ida missed Kate tremendously and would have loved nothing more than a chance to sit down and talk over tea about all that had happened since she'd left the Gulf Coast to return to Georgia. Her brother interrupted her thoughts.

"Hey, sis, why don't you two come by our place for lunch on the way home?"

"Sounds good." Ida accepted the invitation as she and Vivian headed toward their buggy. "We'll meet you there."

Vivian snapped the reins, urging the pony to head toward the roadway. "Well, how'd I do?"

"You were a big hit, I think." Ida hooked her arm through Vivian's.

"Good. I felt like this was sort of our debut. I wanted to make a good impression for you."

"You were perfect. This is perfect." Ida leaned her head on Vivian's shoulder. "I'm so happy that it scares me a little."

Vivian leaned over and kissed the top of Ida's head. "I know what you mean."

Late in the afternoon, Vivian sat on their porch reflecting on the day. She knew it was important for Ida to introduce her to the community at large. Did that mean that their relationship had moved to some new level? She was unsure, but somehow she thought it had. Vivian felt settled in a way she would have never thought possible. Maybe settled was the wrong word. It was more that she felt content. She couldn't remember the last time she'd been in a place or time where contentment descended over her in the way it had recently. She smiled to herself as she propped her boot up on the porch railing in front of her and leaned back in the rocker.

"What are you smiling about?"

Apparently, Ida had been watching her from the doorway for a few minutes.

"Nothing. And everything." Vivian dropped her foot and signaled for Ida to join her. "Come here."

Ida settled into Vivian's lap, wrapped her arms around Vivian's neck, and kissed her affectionately. "Thank you for today."

"You don't need to thank me for being with you." Vivian couldn't help but begin to feel aroused with Ida's hips pressed against her lap. She brought Ida's hand to her lips and kissed her palm.

"I'm practicing gratitude in my daily life." Ida brushed her fingers through Vivian's hair and kissed her forehead. "It's chilly out here. Aren't you ready to come inside?"

"I'm not so chilly now. You're keeping me warm." Vivian nuzzled Ida's neck playfully.

"Your nose is cold!" Ida pushed off her lap and reached back to tug Vivian indoors. "Come inside, I'll make you some hot tea."

As Ida fussed at the stove, preparing to heat some water, Vivian stepped up behind her. She placed her hands on Ida's hips and kissed the back of her neck softly. "There are other things we could do to warm up, you know."

"Is that so?"

Ida reached back and pulled Vivian's mouth firmly against her neck, leaning into Vivian's body. She shivered as she felt Vivian's chilled fingers loosen the fastener at the back of her dress and slowly release each button down to her waist. As Vivian pushed the fabric apart to reveal the slip underneath, Ida felt delicate kisses on the back of her neck and across her shoulders, sending chills down her arms. Her nipples were so hard they ached against the fabric that Vivian was slowly pushing aside. Once the dress had been pushed off her shoulders and down to her waist, the slip was next. Vivian kissed Ida's shoulders as she slipped the narrow satin strap off to the side and swept it down her arms.

"I love the way your skin feels," Vivian murmured against the delicate arc of her shoulder.

Ida pulled her arms free from the top of her dress and slip that now gathered at her hips. She filled her fingers with Vivian's hair, pulling her lips against her neck again. A need was building between her legs with force as she felt Vivian's arms encircle her waist and her strong hands move up her stomach to cover her aching breasts. Ida collapsed against Vivian as she felt her tease and massage.

"Oh, Vivian." She turned in Vivian's arms and pulled her into a deep, luxurious kiss. This was the perfect end to a perfect day.

The notion of tea forgotten, Vivian pulled Ida toward the bedroom. Vivian tugged Ida on top of her. Vivian was still fully dressed even though she'd managed to partially disrobe Ida in the kitchen.

"Ida, you're so pretty." Vivian kissed and caressed her as they lay on top of the covers. Ida shivered under Vivian's touch. "Are you cold?"

"It's not the cold that's making me shiver." Ida slid to the side so that she could push her clothing off and onto the floor; she was now fully nude lying on top of Vivian. She began to work at Vivian's belt and the buttons at the waist of her trousers, all the while keeping Vivian engaged in a fierce kiss. Ida pushed her hand inside Vivian's trousers and began to stroke back and forth, causing Vivian to moan against her mouth.

Ida loved the power she felt over Vivian's desire. Her own arousal grew as she stoked the flame of Vivian's. She felt Vivian move a hand between them and push inside her. Their orgasm was building in unison until, moments later, it exploded.

Vivian wanted Ida again only moments after their first climax. Almost roughly, she tossed Ida onto her back and quickly shucked off her clothes. Ida had slipped under the covers and now lay watching Vivian quickly strip down. Ida's cheeks were flushed and her hair had been loosed from its clasp. Her delicious pink lips were swollen, ready to be taken again. Vivian jerked the covering away from her. She wanted to feel their heat surrounded by the crisp, cool air.

She pushed Ida's legs farther apart as she slid her hips between them. As she slid up, she tried to run her lips over every inch of skin between Ida's hips and her mouth, at last settling into a searing kiss.

"This feels so good. Ida, you make me want to have my mouth on every inch of you."

Something was different. Maybe it was that publicly declaring their coupling in some way gave Vivian hope that this was actually real. They were going to be together. Maybe Ida was falling in love with her. Vivian knew in her heart that she was in love with Ida. She somehow wanted Ida to feel this as intensely as she did. Vivian knew she was being a little rougher than usual, a bit more forceful with need, but it was as if some wild thing inside of her had been set free to roam the landscape of Ida's soft form.

Beneath her, Ida squirmed and arched into her hand as she moved her open palm down Ida's neck, across her breast, and in one fluid move, thrust inside her.

"I want you so badly. Come for me…That's it…" Vivian pressed her full weight on top of Ida as she moved in and out while still exploring Ida's upper body with her mouth. She felt Ida grab fistfuls of hair. Vivian interpreted this as a signal to continue rather than relent.

"Oh, Vivian, oh God—" Ida's words were cut short as Vivian brought her to climax.

"Don't stop." Vivian rode Ida's thigh so that her orgasm quickly followed Ida's. As she collapsed on top of Ida, she felt Ida peppering her with kisses all about her face and neck.

Ida shuddered with post orgasmic tremors. "Vivian, you're an amazing lover." Vivian was still inside her. Ida wrapped her leg over Vivian's hips, holding her in place as small orgasms continued to ripple through Ida's entire body.

Sensing that Ida was still quite aroused, Vivian began to slowly caress inside with her fingers. "Is this okay?" She raised up on her elbow so that she could look into Ida's bottomless blue eyes.

"Yes, more…"

"As much as you want. I could do this forever."

Maybe just getting to the Blue Mountains wasn't enough. Maybe that wasn't all that there was. Maybe Ida was what made Vivian feel whole. Place alone would not answer all of Vivian's need.

Vivian kissed Ida's swollen lips as she continued the caress between her legs. "Ida, I'm so in love with you." She felt Ida's nails dig into her shoulders as the orgasm claimed her again.

Vivian could see tears gathered at her lashes as Ida pulled away to look into her face. "I love you, too. So much."

CHAPTER THIRTY-SIX

The autumn air was brisk and arid. Golden poplars and red maples dotted the hillsides around the farm, interspersed with orange and brown oaks.

Sensations of Ida underneath her the previous afternoon stayed with Vivian as she began her day's chores. She shuddered just thinking about the feeling of Ida's soft curves pressed warmly against her. Vivian fought her arousal as she hitched the horse to the plow and walked out toward the field. She had told Samuel the previous day she was strong enough to guide the plow behind the mare and turn the field in preparation for the next planting season. As they reached the edge of the plot, Vivian lowered the till point into the earth, draped the reins around her good shoulder, and snapped the leather straps resting on the horse's back to get her moving forward. There had been little rain, so the dirt was stiff and hard. This could make for a long day.

Still buried in her own thoughts, Vivian lost track of how long she'd been behind the plow until she saw Samuel heading in her direction. As she halted the horse and looked up at the sky she realized it was past noon. Sweat had drenched her shirt, and her arms ached.

"Hello there!" called Samuel as he approached.

"Hello!" Vivian wiped sweat off her forehead with her shirtsleeve.

"You are a woman on a mission out here," said Samuel. He stepped close to where Vivian was leaning on the plow. "Rachel said you didn't take a break for lunch so I thought I'd best come check on you. This doesn't all have to be done today, you know."

"Yeah, I guess I was a little lost in thought. And then lost track of time, but I'm feeling it in my arms now."

"Why don't I take a turn? I'll make a few more passes, then we'll call it a day and give the horse a break, too." Samuel adjusted his wide-brimmed hat to offer his eyes a bit more shade.

"Maybe you're right." Vivian lifted the reins from around her shoulder and passed them to Samuel. "I might be done for the day anyway. My stamina isn't quite back to normal yet."

"Well, I'm glad I came to find you then. Take a break and we'll see you later. We should all have dinner together again soon."

"Yeah, definitely." Vivian smiled at Samuel as she walked in the direction of Ida's house. She thought she'd eat a little food, clean up, and change shirts. She might even take a nap. Then she'd be good and rested when Ida returned home from her trip to the village mill.

❖

The sun was high in the sky as Ida trekked to the mill. Had there been a town center, the mill would have been located just at the far end of Main Street. There really was no town, but instead more of a collection of wooden and stone structures facing out along a dirt road that lead up to the old stone community-run gristmill.

A village of structures, used for a common purpose. Most of the buildings served as open markets where local residents could trade and barter for goods. Honey was traded for cloth, handwoven blankets were traded for birch wood baskets, along with a wide assortment of other handmade goods. Transient workers would sometimes lounge about the front of the buildings and hire themselves out for a day's labor in trade for food and sometimes lodging.

Ida traveled past the market buildings and headed toward the mill. As she passed she waved at people she knew and gave them a smile and a "good day." It was nice to be home surrounded by familiar faces that belonged to folks Ida had known her entire life. She didn't regret her time away; in fact, she felt certain time and distance had only served to help her appreciate the familiar. There was comfort in being known.

As Ida and her horse-drawn buggy approached, she idly wondered who was running the mill today. There wasn't much to running the old mill. The stream did all the real work, as long as there was enough rain so that the water passing through the sluice gate carried the necessary volume to turn the large vertical water wheel that operated the pit wheel and subsequently the actual milling stone. When the mill was open, someone had to manually operate the sluice and close it when the mill shut down for the day. Farmers from all over the area brought their grain to this mill so that it could be ground and bagged as flour. In the winter months, cornbread was a staple of the local diet so it was important to keep the mill working as regularly as possible.

It was still early in the afternoon, and it looked as if Ida might be the only customer at the moment. She pulled up next to the old stone building and stepped down from the high seat that squeaked loudly as she moved off and dropped to the ground. She lifted the sack of dried corn from the back of the buggy and headed toward the mill's dark interior.

The mill was located on a rise along a wide stream, which could almost be considered a river, overlooking several valley farms at a slightly lower elevation. The thick stone walls captured and held the dampness of the creek as it passed through. During certain months, feathery moss gathered on the rough rock walls nearest the wood-sided sluice. This damp microclimate kept the summer temperatures quite cool within the dark interior of the mill, and in the winter, it was downright frigid. As she stepped through the small stone entryway, Ida noticed the smell of the damp earthen floor hanging in the air.

It took a few seconds for Ida's vision to adjust to the dark interior. She heard the sound of movement. To her left, she could see someone silhouetted against one of the small windows that made a feeble attempt at shedding light inside the building. Ida recognized her right away, and a knot in her stomach followed that realization.

"Hi, Chris." There was no way to avoid the encounter with her ex, so Ida decided just to push through it. They were the only two in the place, and that meant that Chris was running the mill for the day. If she wanted to get the corn ground, she'd have to suffer through whatever Chris had to say while she waited for the grinding stone to do its work.

Chris moved away from the window so that the large grinding mechanism was between where she stood and the opening where Ida stood, just inside the door frame. Chris was of average height with a square build. Her dark hair was cropped short, her plaid shirt tucked into boxy trousers, with the sleeves rolled to the elbows. Chris gave Ida a look that was hard to read. Maybe she was trying to go for neutral, but she instead just looked annoyed.

"Ida, what a surprise." Although Chris didn't really seem surprised. She came close to Ida and acted as if she might give her a hug, but she could obviously read Ida's body language, so she stopped herself.

"I'm sorry. If I'd known this was your day at the mill I wouldn't have come." Ida moved from the doorway and stepped inside, still holding the ten-pound sack of corn.

Ida couldn't pinpoint exactly what it was about Chris's manner that set her nerves on edge, but it was hard to ignore the tension hanging in the air between them. They hadn't parted on the best of terms. Ida had left Chris and moved back home to care for her mother. Chris had assumed that Ida would come back to her after her mother's death, and when she hadn't, Chris was less than pleased. She'd always tried to control Ida when they'd lived together, and when she couldn't coerce Ida into moving back in with her she'd gotten pretty angry. Chris's inability to let go had contributed to Ida's reasons for leaving and traveling south with Kate and her husband.

"I'm glad you're here. We were bound to run into each other sooner or later." Chris scuffed the dirt with the toe of her boot and shoved her hands in her pockets. "I wanted to see you. If I hadn't run into you soon I was going to swing by your place."

Ida cringed at the thought that Chris might have shown up while Vivian was still recovering. "I'd prefer if you didn't just stop by, Chris. It's probably not a good idea."

"Yeah, I heard you brought some stranger back with you from down south. I heard she's staying in your house with you."

So much for appreciating the familiar. It obviously hadn't taken long for Chris to find out what was going on in her life, whether she chose to share the news or not. "You make it sound like I brought home a stray."

"Isn't that what you did?" Chris reached to take the bag of grain from Ida and moved to empty it in the trough in front of the slow-moving grinding stone. The thick-timbered spokes creaked as the large round stone followed its circular grinding path.

"I don't really want to discuss my personal life with you, Chris. I don't need your permission or approval for what I do in my own house." Ida wasn't sure why she let Chris get to her. They hadn't seen each other in over a year, and it had taken less than five minutes for Chris to cause Ida's temper to flare. She knew if she lingered to wait for the corn meal they would get into a fight, so she made an excuse to leave. "I need to go down and see the healer about some medicine," Ida lied. "I'll come back in a little while to pick this up."

"I could bring it out to your place later. There's no need for you to come back and get it."

"Thank you for the offer, but it won't take long with Francis. I'll be back."

"I'll bring this by your house." Chris made the statement as if Ida hadn't just told her she wasn't welcome to come by the house. She clearly wasn't listening.

Ida had been trying to make her escape, but after hearing the self-assured declaration from Chris, she spun on her heels. "I said

I'd come back for the corn meal and that's exactly what I'll do. I don't want you to bring it to the house."

"Okay, okay, no need to get so defensive." Chris's patronizing tone flew against Ida's heated cheeks like a brisk wind.

"I'm not being defensive, Chris. I've just told you that you aren't welcome at my house and you act like you can just bully your way back into my life." Ida had stepped closer to Chris so that even in the low light of the mill's interior Chris wouldn't be able to miss the look of frustration that was no doubt present on her face.

"Okay, I get it." Chris took a step back.

"Do you? Do you ever really listen? Did you ever really listen even when we were together?" This might have been the first time Ida had really stood up to Chris's controlling nature. When they'd split up it'd been easier just to leave than to continue arguing. Standing up to Chris felt good. She hesitated, waiting for Chris to respond, and when no response was delivered she turned and exited the mill.

Ida shook her head as she walked down the hill toward Francis's office. *How did I ever let myself get into a relationship with her in the first place? Unbelievable.*

As she walked she had a realization of how different things were with Vivian. Her relationship with Vivian was more equal. Obviously, she and Vivian were very different but their oppositeness only seemed to enrich who they were together. She smiled as she imagined a future with Vivian. A future with Vivian had unlimited possibility because Vivian would never try to hold her back or control her the way Chris had done. She knew with certainty that Vivian wanted Ida to be her own person and would allow her the space to have her own dreams.

Ida's chest expanded with a sense of love and rightness. She would do everything in her power to make a go of things with Vivian. They were good together and she realized now that goodness should be cherished and nurtured.

She hoped Francis was in. If not, she'd have to figure out some other way to waste time until the grain was finished. She wasn't going to get forced into some other tense argument with Chris. That would just ruin her whole day. As thoughts of Vivian filled her mind the day was just looking brighter and brighter and she didn't want anything to wreck her fine mood.

CHAPTER THIRTY-SEVEN

Vivian looked out at the clouds growing heavier and more foreboding by the minute and realized she was glad she'd come in from the field early. She'd washed up and was finger-combing her damp hair as she walked out onto the porch. The air was so thick with humidity that her clean shirt was already plastered to her back. A flash of lightning ripped across the sky; a booming rumble quickly followed. Vivian's scalp tingled and her forearm prickled as the small hairs on her skin rose with the static electricity in the air. *Damn, that was close.* Apprehension gathered and crept through her mind. It hadn't yet begun to rain, but the deep purple-gray of the boiling cumulus overhead signaled its approach. Her thoughts went to Ida, and how her pony would certainly be spooked by the thunder if she was now on her way back from the village.

Vivian scanned the sky again, her eyes settling on a particularly furious dark cloud. She frowned. That wasn't a cloud. That was smoke coming from Rachel and Samuel's place! She leapt off the porch and started across the field between the two houses as fast as she could run. Her movements were slowed by the soft ridges of piled soil. Vivian was sinking almost up to her ankles in some places, stumbling over clods of dirt, and cursing. This suspended moment was like one of those dreams where you were running and running, but you couldn't get to where you need to be in time. Apprehension filled her chest.

As she got closer, Vivian could see that the smoke billowed from the old wooden barn. Vivian ran through a quick list of items that couldn't be lost in the fire. The doors swung wide open and a dark column of smoke licked from the high opening of the hayloft and the eaves. One of the horses burst past her and out the large door, knocking her over. Scrambling to her feet, she heard hooves drumming against wood in the back of the barn. Straining to peer through the smoke, she realized Rachel was in the barn, trying to free the second horse. Vivian's heart pummeled in her chest as she looked up to see flames licking overhead, the loft fully engulfed, the air full of smoke. When she reached the back of the barn, the mare was kicking and turning panicked circles in her stall. She was whinnying, calling to the other horse that'd already made his escape. Rachel opened the stall door, but the mare was focused on the flames skimming along the ceiling overhead and the burning hay raining down. Vivian lunged for a blanket. By the time she got to the stall, Rachel had a hand on the mare's halter and was holding on for dear life. Vivian threw the blanket over the frantic horse's head. It stilled, trembling while they tucked the blanket into her halter. As Vivian lowered the blanket, she could see the orange glow from the flames just outside the stall reflected in the glassy pools of the horse's frantic eyes. The searing heat inside the structure was so intense that it seemed to suck the oxygen right from Vivian's lungs.

"Vivian! Thank God. I couldn't get her to move."

"We need to get out of here! The fire is spreading too fast!" The crackling of the flames almost drowned out her voice. Vivian tried to soothe the frightened animal as they moved toward the door.

"Rachel! I've got this, get out!" Rachel was at the horse's flank, strangling on the smoke-filled air. "Rachel!"

But Rachel couldn't hear Vivian over the roar of the fire. Timbers aged and thick with long-trapped resin now popped and sizzled from the heat all around them.

As the mare neared the door, Vivian let the blanket fall away as the horse bolted from the flaming structure. Rachel was nowhere in sight. Panic choked Vivian's throat as badly as the smoke. She forced herself to march back into the burning barn. Rachel was heading toward the door, dragging a harness and a heavy plow collar, visibly struggling under the weight of the gear. Vivian took the equipment from her. She veered toward the open door and sprinted for safety, hoping to God all the while that Rachel was following her.

The searing heat pressed against her tender flesh without even touching it, so great was the temperature inside the flaming structure. Vivian lurched as the ground shifted under her feet. Almost at the same instant she fell, Vivian heard a thunderous crack. The ground trembled as a huge section of the barn's upper level came crashing down all around her. She had fallen near the large front opening of the barn, but even with the fresh air so close, Vivian was fighting to breathe. Her eyes burned and she was coughing furiously. Just when Vivian needed saving, strong hands grasped at her under her arms and pulled her toward the open door. Clinging to the tack and collar, she pulled them along to safety.

Samuel knelt down beside her. "Vivian, are you all right? I saw the smoke. I got here as fast as I could from the far field." Between the run and the smoke, Samuel was gasping for air.

"Rachel!" Vivian rasped and coughed. She pointed toward the barn's flaming interior.

Samuel didn't hesitate. He charged into the smoke and fire-infested barn, leaving Vivian lying in the dirt, gasping for breath.

❖

As the sky began to darken earlier than usual, Ida decided she should get herself home ahead of the storm that seemed to be moving in. She was almost there when the first bolt of lightning flared and then boomed. Her pony skittered and snorted, spooked by both the flash and the noise. Ida tried to calm the pony but then the second strike sounded, louder than the first. The second hit was so loud that even Ida was startled.

A north to south wind had picked up considerably in the past half hour and the temperature dropped. Ida pulled her coat more tightly around her with one hand as she snapped the reins again with the other. As they rounded the last turn in the rutted dirt road that emptied out into the far corner of their farm, Ida saw a long, thick plume of smoke coming from the direction of the barn. Panic struck through her chest. *No, no, no!* Leaning forward on the wooden plank seat of the buggy, Ida took the leather straps in both hands and slapped them sharply on the pony's back.

❖

Vivian was getting to her knees when a burst of movement caught her eye. Cole! She was running headlong after her father. Cole crossed the threshold of the flaming barn before Vivian managed to grab her arm. Vivian snagged her and hoisted her away from the blaze.

"Daddy! Mama!" Cole writhed frenetically as she fought to free herself from Vivian's grasp. Vivian could sense the child's panic as if it were her own. In this moment of connection it was hard to tell the difference.

It seemed like an eternity, but it had likely been only seconds since Samuel had run back in after Rachel. As Vivian continued her fight to restrain her, a deafening crunch sounded behind them as heavy timbers in the center of the wooden structure buckled and gave way, sending sparks, flames, and huge plumes of black smoke skyward.

"Noooooo!" Cole wailed.

Vivian cradled Cole's face against her shoulder, her tears soaking through Vivian's soot-covered shirt. She faced them away from the collapsing inferno. Vivian turned back for a second, while shielding Cole's view, to see the remaining struts of the building collapse inward and flame up like a huge pyre. The temperature was so intense Vivian staggered backward as the heat pulsed over her in waves.

"Vivian!"

Ida ran toward them as her terrified gaze focused on the disaster unfolding in front of them. Soothing arms enveloped her waist as Ida attempted to capture both Vivian and Cole in her arms. Cole turned and reached for Ida. As Ida pulled Cole close, she turned to Vivian with her eyes full of tears.

"Samuel?"

Vivian shook her head.

"Rachel?" Ida's voice broke.

Vivian shook her head again and shut her eyes. The pain on Ida's face was more than she could suffer. As if it were her own, as if some strange entity had reached into her chest clenching its fist around her heart. There was nothing to be done now and no one left to save. Rachel and Samuel were lost to them.

Vivian paced. She turned to see Ida crying into Cole's neck as the dry, crumbled timbers continued to burn hotly in front of them. Through her tears, Vivian watched the wind swallow the billowing black smoke swarm as it climbed into the storm-darkened sky. As she watched the dark column taken up by the wind, she heard her grandfather's voice. *The wind receives our first breath and our last sigh.*

❖

It was hard to know what to do or how long to linger as the rain came and the embers sizzled and steamed long after sunset. Ida took Cole to her house. Vivian watched them walk away, exhausted and heartbroken. Cole's chin rested on Ida's shoulder as she carried her home. She seemed to look back at Vivian with empty eyes.

Vivian remained a few moments longer by the destroyed barn. It seemed too soon to leave the site where she'd last seen Rachel and Samuel. The rain soaked through Vivian's shirt, and rivulets ran down her neck and inside her shirt collar. After a while, after the cold badly enveloped her body, she turned and walked toward the house. Soggy soil clung to her boots, making her steps labored and slow, as if echoing the burden of sadness she carried on her shoulders. If she'd only gotten to the barn sooner. If she'd only been able to stop Rachel from going back inside. If. If. If.

Vivian stepped out of her boots on the porch and moved into the low light of the main room where Ida sat with Cole.

"Get out!" Cole strained against Ida, pointing her finger at Vivian who stood ghostlike just inside the entryway. "She can't be in here!"

"Cole! Stop. Why would you say such a thing?" asked Ida.

"I could have saved them. She stopped me! It's her fault."

"Cole, it was a fire. An accident. It was no one's fault," said Ida.

"She can't come in here!"

"I'll just wait on the porch."

Vivian stepped back outside as Ida gave her a pained look. She took a seat in an old rocker on the porch and listened through the open door as Ida tried to soothe Cole. It took a while longer for the child to settle down enough that Ida could put her to bed.

Gentle fingers brushed along Vivian's shoulder when she realized she'd been lost in thought.

"I'm so sorry, Vivian. She's just confused and angry. You didn't deserve that."

"She didn't deserve what happened today either. No one did."

Vivian believed that chaos was a part of the natural world and that it was important to be able to tolerate a certain amount of chaos, which she'd always interpreted as the world's tendency toward unfairness. This would be one of those times. But her tolerance was maxed out. She wished she was also a child so she could rage against God and ask for answers, but she knew the Great Spirit held its own counsel. She doubted even if she demanded them that answers would come.

CHAPTER THIRTY-EIGHT

A s was the custom, the women came and brought food for those who mourned. The men from nearby farms came to help with the cleanup and the burial of the remains. The next day, as if to mock them, the weather was beautiful. The sky was clear and blue as the mourners gathered at the sites of the graves set one beside the other in the small family plot at the edge of the George property. As each person left, they solemnly tossed a handful of dark soil onto the wooden boxes deep set into the earth, one for Samuel and one for Rachel. A lone female voice, soulful and earnest, sang the graveside service's closing hymn. *Softly, tenderly Jesus is calling. Come home, come home.*

Standing next to Ida and Cole, Vivian placed her hand on Cole's shoulder only to have it shaken off as Cole gave her a dark look before running away from them.

"She doesn't mean it." Ida took Vivian's hand in hers.

"I think she might."

Cole was angry and Vivian could hardly blame her. Since there was no one or no thing to target with her rage, she had chosen to place it on Vivian. In her child logic, Vivian reasoned, she was the one who'd held Cole back and kept her from saving her parents. Cole had said as much the first night, hours after the fire when they had tried to get her to sleep.

All that was left now was to cover the plain wooden boxes that held the remains of Ida's brother and his sweet wife.

"You go be with Cole. I can stay and help with this."

Vivian meant to stay and help James and Ben shovel dirt to close the graves. Both men had been incredibly thoughtful and helpful since the horrific accident.

Ida nodded to Vivian and allowed their fingers to drift apart as she walked after Cole, who'd headed back toward the house. Ida had spent a small amount of time moving a few of Cole's things over to her house in the hopes that she'd be more at ease. But Vivian knew it was going to take more than a few items of clothing and toys to soothe Cole's anger over what had just happened.

The sound of loose soil echoed on top of the wooden boxes. Vivian reached for the shovel buried in the dirt pile next to her, standing as if at attention. Mimicking the somber movements of the two men next to her, she joined them in replacing the upturned dirt back onto the graves.

Funerals were sad events to be sure, but nothing made the passing of a loved one as real or absolute as shoveling the dirt over their coffin. *Ashes to ashes. Dust to dust.* If it was possible that such a menial task could be done with reverence, that was what the three of them attempted. As Vivian pivoted with the shovel, each time filling it with the dark earth, she thought of her grandfather and how she missed him. *The earth does not belong to man; man belongs to the earth.* These days his words seemed to resurface in her mind more often. As her experiences had expanded, his messages resonated with her more than they ever had when her world was small, before she left Oklahoma.

As they finished, Ben gathered the shovels and began walking toward his wagon, leaving James and Vivian standing alone for a few minutes. Vivian had never had a sibling. She could only guess at the grief Ida was feeling over the loss of her brother. A man that Vivian felt she barely got the chance to know.

"I found this."

Vivian extended her palm to receive a soot-covered pocket watch, the crystal cracked in two places, no doubt from the heat of the fire. "This was Samuel's watch."

Vivian rolled the watch over in her hand and looked up to James's eyes. "Thank you."

"He would want Cole to have it. When she's ready."

"I'll keep it for her until then."

James nodded and pulled on his hat, lowering it over his eyes. Vivian cradled the watch in her hand as she watched James's slow retreat.

CHAPTER THIRTY-NINE

Several days after the fire, Ida thought maybe she should look through the things in Samuel's house. There would be clothes to disperse to folks who might be in need. There were other household goods that could be bartered for what they might need around the farm. There was equipment that had been lost in the fire that would need to be replaced, and Ida would have to figure out a way to replace it.

All of these and more were the mundane tasks of the living that remained after the loss of loved ones. Since the fire, Ida had gone back to the house only once to collect some things for Cole, but she was having a difficult time mustering the emotional fortitude to begin the task of dismantling her brother's life. In truth, she could leave some chores for later, but there were a few things that needed to be dealt with sooner rather than later.

Ida had decided today would be the day to take some of those first steps toward dealing with things in the house. As she approached, she noticed the front door was open. She glanced around and saw that Vivian was far across the field, near the back of the springhouse.

Ida approached the open door with caution. It wasn't unheard of to be visited by scavengers looking for food or other things if a house looked uninhabited. If anyone had been watching the place they'd have plainly seen no activity for several days.

The timbers of the front steps creaked as she put her full weight on them. She hesitated between steps and listened but heard no sound coming from the house. She stepped across the threshold and listened again. Nothing.

And then as she moved farther into the interior she heard it, a muffled sound coming from the main bedroom. Stepping as lightly as possible, Ida approached the bedroom door and leaned in through the doorway.

Her stomach clenched at what she saw.

Cole was standing in the closet, with her mother's clothes gathered into her arms, crying. Her face was buried into the folds of hanging fabric and her back was toward the door so she didn't know she'd been discovered.

Witnessing this moment of private grief gripped Ida's chest like a clenched fist. She covered her mouth to smother the sob that rose quickly in her throat and backed out of the house. Once she was in the front yard, she began walking in slow circles taking deep breaths in attempt to settle her tears. She brushed them away with the back of her hand as she paced back and forth in front of the porch steps.

She looked at the open door, considering what she should do. Was it better to allow Cole this moment alone or should she go try and console her? Ida wasn't sure what the right thing to do was. She wanted to allow Cole to grieve in her own way, but she also wanted Cole to know that she could turn to Ida when she needed comfort.

After a few moments of deliberation, Ida decided to go back inside. Cole was still holding on to an armful of her mother's dresses as Ida approached.

She put her hand gently on Cole's back and knelt down beside her.

"Cole, sweetheart, why don't you come sit with me?" She rubbed slow circles on Cole's back.

"I miss her so much," Cole said through muffled sobbing sounds.

"I know you do."

"Her clothes still smell like her."

Ida's heart ached, it thumped in her chest, dull and heavy. "Come here, baby."

Cole partially turned and Ida pulled her into her arms. Cole leaned into her, throwing her arms around Ida's neck.

"Everything is going to be okay, Cole. I know it hurts now, but it will get easier, I promise."

"I don't think it will."

"I know you don't right now, but it will. And until it does, you don't have to be sad alone, okay? You can always come find me, okay?"

She felt Cole nod against her shoulder.

❖

Vivian had seen Ida pacing in front of the house. Something about the way Ida was moving worried her and so she'd crossed the field to investigate. She'd entered the house after Ida and quietly watched from the bedroom door as Cole and Ida embraced. She heard them talking in hushed tones but couldn't make out what they were saying.

Ida looked in her direction but she couldn't read her expression. Did Ida want her to stay or go?

She felt like an outsider. And not wanting to intrude, she turned and swiftly exited the house. She hadn't meant to interrupt this intimate family moment.

Even though she and Ida had professed their love for each other, she wasn't family and Cole was still angry with her for what had happened the day of the fire. Vivian was at a loss as she stood with arms crossed on the porch.

After a few minutes, she heard footsteps. Cole stepped past her and, without speaking, she ran down the steps and back toward Ida's house. She'd given Vivian a scowl before making her escape across the front lawn.

After another moment, Ida stepped out onto the porch beside her.

"I don't know what to do to help her." Ida hugged herself as she stood beside Vivian watching Cole's figure retreat.

"She just needs time." She reached to touch Ida, but then didn't. She shoved her hand in her pocket instead.

"I just don't know. I feel that I'm as sad as she is. I'm no help." Ida turned toward Vivian, her eyes red rimmed.

Vivian wanted to say something consoling, something wise, something. But nothing came. Instead selfish thoughts rose to the surface.

How could she leave Ida now even if she wanted to? She'd told Ida she loved her and she knew she did, but had she meant she would stay? Ida needed her; whether she wanted her or not, she certainly needed her now. The sensation of feeling trapped crept over Vivian like a slowly lengthening shadow cast by the setting sun. Tightness settled into her chest. She sensed that Ida was looking at her, waiting for her to say something, but she couldn't look at her.

"I've got a bit more to do. I'll come to the house later." She turned and walked away from Ida without looking back.

CHAPTER FORTY

Two months had passed since the day of the fire. It seemed now that life was organized by what happened before the fire and what happened after the fire. As if all order was reset by that single, catastrophic event. Thanksgiving was almost upon them. It would be hard to be in the spirit of the season given all that had been lost so recently. Thanks seemed elusive.

Vivian had done her best to comfort Ida. In truth, they had grown much closer over the past several weeks. Every now and then, doubts still crept up on Vivian and she wondered if she was worthy of the trust Ida seemed to place in her.

The leaves were all gone from the trees now, leaving them stripped and bare against the gray sky of the approaching winter. Vivian had put all her efforts into getting them ready for the cold season—curing venison, storing potatoes and other root vegetables, along with the canned goods that Rachel and Ida had finished just before Rachel's death. It would be with a heavy heart that those apples were consumed as jam or baked into pies.

Cole continued to struggle to come to terms with the loss of her parents. She was still angry but not so much at Vivian anymore. Her admiration had returned somewhat as Vivian tried to help her with distractions around the farm. She was teaching Cole to shoot with the bow, and she seemed to have a natural affinity for it. Vivian could see that Cole would one day be quite a gifted marksman. They had worked together to craft a smaller bow for Cole to practice with. Even the shafts of the arrows had been shortened and carried only wooden tips so that she could do limited damage.

Ida watched Vivian walk toward the house one chilly afternoon, having just given Cole another shooting lesson. Cole had stayed out in the pasture to practice. She was to shoot at a straw target, retrieve her arrow, and shoot again. Vivian made slow progress back toward the house, turning every so often to glance back in Cole's direction. Vivian was wearing a heavy wool coat against the cold breeze that had arrived. Ida pulled her sweater more tightly around her as Vivian neared the porch steps.

"How is she today?"

"Every day she gets a little better." Vivian scuffed mud off her boots as she climbed the steps. "I'll have to take these off before I come in."

Some days were better for Ida than others. Today was not one of those better days. She'd come across one of Samuel's old felt hats in the back of a closet, and the sight of it had triggered a dull ache in her chest. Losing her older brother felt like losing her anchor in the world. She relied on him. She counted on having him nearby as they grew together into old age. Without him, she was afraid she wouldn't be able to keep the farm. Ida worried she'd be no better off than Rebecca had been after she'd lost her husband, Eric. Plus, now she was left to raise a child that she'd only just reconnected with after being away for more than a year.

But what worried Ida the most, the thing that kept her up late into the night after everyone else was asleep, was the fear that Vivian was only staying now because she felt pity for Ida. Vivian hadn't said anything to that effect, but Ida's fears held sway nonetheless. As Vivian stepped up onto the landing next to her, Ida lost her battle with tears. She wiped at them with the hopes of shooing them away before Vivian could see them glistening on her cheeks.

"Hey, what's that about? What's wrong?" Vivian put her hands on Ida's arms and bent down to meet Ida's gaze.

"Nothing, I'm fine."

"Come on, talk to me. Aren't you the one who is always telling me to talk about my feelings?"

Ida couldn't help smiling through her tears. "Yes, and I hate the way you always remember what I say to you."

"No, you don't."

"You're right. I don't." Ida sniffed and wiped away another tear with the palm of her hand.

"So what is it? Please tell me so that I don't worry." Vivian pulled Ida into the warmth of her coat and Ida gratefully snuggled under Vivian's chin.

"I'm worried that you're only staying because you feel sorry for me. And how could you not when I've been feeling so sorry for myself?" She felt Vivian kiss the top of her head. "With all that's gone on, how can I know the real reason you've stayed?" She pulled back to look up into Vivian's eyes. "And now I have a child to raise. It's too much. It's not fair for you to inherit an instant family...a woman and a child that isn't yours."

They'd been concentrating so keenly on each other that neither of them had noticed Cole's approach until it was too late. Ida saw her, but only after she'd already made the statement about Vivian raising a child that wasn't hers. Cole looked crestfallen. She hesitated for only a moment before she turned and ran toward the tree line.

"Cole! Wait!" Ida broke free from Vivian's embrace and yelled after her. She leapt off the porch to follow her, but Vivian stopped her, seeing that Ida wasn't dressed warm enough for the chill.

"I'll go. Cole and I need to talk some things over and it's long overdue."

"Are you sure?"

"I'm sure." Vivian pulled Ida into a kiss. "And when I get back, you and I will talk some more, okay?" She cupped Ida's face between her hands. "Everything is going to be okay." Ida nodded, tears beginning to fall slowly down her cheeks again. "Now get inside before you get too cold. I'll be back shortly with Cole."

Vivian smiled over her shoulder as she trotted in Cole's footsteps. She didn't catch up to her, but in the dry, partly frozen grass and dirt, it was easy to follow her trail. Cole ran pretty far before Vivian finally spotted her. She had traveled maybe a mile from the boundary of the farm, up the ridge, and was seated on the steps at the base of what looked like some sort of old lookout tower.

Cole was drawing shapes in the dirt with a stick when Vivian sat down next to her.

"This is a pretty interesting place." Vivian looked up the steps toward the landing that wrapped around the entire upper structure.

"It's an old fire tower," Cole mumbled, resting her chin in her hand, propped on her knee.

"Is it? I've never been in a fire tower."

"I'm gonna live here one day."

"Well, your house will have a great view then."

They sat silently for a few minutes. Cole didn't look at Vivian, but instead continued moving the tip of her stick around in the loose dirt near their feet. Finally, she spoke. "Are you gonna leave because of me?"

"I'm not leaving, Cole."

"But I heard what Aunt Ida said. She said having a kid to raise is too much."

"Cole, I know that you've been really upset, but try and think about all the ways that Ida is upset, too." Vivian rested her arms on her knees as she spoke, quietly, in an even tone. "You and I have never had a brother, so we don't know what it feels like to lose one. Ida really misses her brother. She's scared without him, I think." Vivian reached for a stick and began to mimic Cole's drawings in the dirt until Cole stopped and looked over at her. "Your aunt loves you very much. You should know that she would do anything for you. What you heard was only part of what she was saying, and none of it was really about you."

Cole was still hurt and angry. "Well, I don't care. I don't need anyone to take care of me anyway."

Vivian figured she and Ida had let Cole's anger simmer long enough. It was time to work on getting her past it.

"Can I tell you a story, Cole? It's a story my grandfather used to tell me when anger settled inside me and wouldn't leave."

"What were you so angry about?"

"I was angry that my mom left me and I never understood why."

"Where did she go?"

"I don't know. One day she just left and didn't come back, and it made me really angry. So angry that even now I still think about it."

"What was the story your granddad told you?" Cole looked at Vivian expectantly.

"An old Cherokee elder was teaching his grandson about life." Vivian looked off into the distant trees, trying to remember all the details of the story that she'd not heard since she was a child seated at her grandfather's knee. "He said a fight is going on inside me. It's a terrible fight and it's between two wolves. One is evil—he is anger, envy, regret, greed, arrogance, resentment, and ego. The other is good—he is joy, peace, love, hope, kindness, empathy, truth, compassion, and faith."

Vivian looked over at Cole, who was listening intently. "This same fight is going on inside you—and inside every other person, too."

"Is that true?"

"Yes, it's true." Vivian leaned forward, resting her elbows on her knees. "So, the grandson thought about it for a minute and then asked his grandfather, which wolf will win? The old man simply replied, the one I feed."

As Vivian finished the story, the impact of her own words settled like a weight in her chest. She realized she'd been talking to Cole, but that she also needed to heed the message she'd just delivered.

"I want to feed the good wolf," said Cole softly.

Vivian put her arm around Cole and pulled her close, "Me, too."

She felt Cole shake beside her as she sobbed quietly against Vivian's side. Vivian leaned over and pressed her lips into Cole's hair. "You're going to be okay, Cole. We all are."

After a little while, the tears subsided, but Cole remained leaning against Vivian.

"Hey, I have something for you." Vivian opened her hand to show Cole the watch. "It was your father's watch. I think he'd want you to have it now."

Cole took the watch, rolling it over in her small fingers. She sniffed again and plunged the large pocket watch into her trousers. "We should probably head back so that Aunt Ida doesn't worry."

"I think that's a good idea."

As they began to walk back toward the farm, Vivian felt Cole slip her tiny hand into hers. That simple gesture of affection caused Vivian's heart to swell. She blamed the cold air for the tears that gathered at the edges of her eyelids, but deep down she knew the reason for their appearance.

They walked hand in hand all the way back to the house. Only when they stepped into the golden grass at the boundary between the road and the farmhouse did Cole release her grip and run toward Ida's pony. Cole's cloud of sadness was set aside for the time being. Vivian stood watching Cole running through the tall, dry grass until she reached the pony and rubbed its neck.

Ida came to stand beside Vivian, watching.

"What did you say to her?" Ida entwined her fingers with Vivian's.

"A story my grandfather used to tell me when I was mad at the world." Vivian turned to regard Ida. "I realized as I was telling it that I needed to hear the story again myself."

"Maybe you'll share it with me sometime?"

Vivian turned to face Ida. The red hue of the sunset reflected against her translucent blue eyes. She stroked Ida's cheek and tucked her favorite errant strand of blond hair behind her ear. "Marry me, dearest Ida."

Ida closed her eyes and smiled, hesitating for just the briefest moment while the words she had so longed to hear washed over her.

"Marry me." Vivian said the words again.

"Yes, my love. I will marry you. Without reservation and with my whole heart."

"I love you, Ida. You must know that I love you because of who you are and because you inspire me to be a better person. I want to stay with you forever. Not because I feel pity for you but because I know that I am nothing without you. You and Cole mean the world to me."

"Oh, Vivian. I love you so much."

They held each other close, standing silhouetted against the reddening sky, sheltered from the hurt of the world, in the refuge of each other's arms. Vivian tilted Ida's face up so that she could kiss her tenderly. As their lips met, she knew in her heart that she had finally found what she'd been searching for. She felt her destiny envelop her in a loving embrace.

EPILOGUE

On the eve of the New Year, Vivian insisted the three of them walk up the ridge to a spot she'd grown attached to. There was a gap at the crest of the ridge, a low place, where a stand of poplars, uniform in size, gathered in a circle as if they were a boundary for some natural cathedral. It was cold and dark, and as they climbed the hill to the ridge, their breath cast before them in white puffs.

When they entered the small open clearing in the midst of the poplar grove, Vivian knelt and began digging a small trench with her hunting knife in the frozen earth. After she had a space she felt was deep enough, she removed her grandfather's map from her coat pocket. She kissed the faded yellow paper and placed it in the freshly dug hole. As Vivian was covering the map with dirt, Cole became distracted by ice crystals pushing up through the dead leaves like tiny crystalline castles, and pulled Ida over to look at them.

Vivian patted the freshly turned dark soil over the now buried map and as she glanced up, she saw the ghostly white shape of her grandfather. For a moment, she held her breath, afraid to move or speak. The spirit of her grandfather smiled and nodded, then slowly turned and disappeared into the thickening forest of the Blue Mountains. She realized no one else had seen him. Vivian smiled and turned to look up at Ida from her kneeling position.

"Are you ready?" Ida extended her hand to Vivian and helped her up.

"I'm ready." Vivian stood and brushed bits of dry leaves off from her knees with her open hand.

"Let's go home," said Ida. She called for Cole to join them.

And for the first time in a very long time, Vivian truly understood the meaning of the word. She knew that home was not a structure with four walls, it wasn't about a geographical place but rather a place where love resided. And that place was with Ida and Cole.

Vivian and Ida linked arms, and Cole's small hand slipped into Vivian's as they began their descent from the crest of the ridge toward the house. Vivian leaned close and spoke softly. "Yes, my sweet love, let's go home."

About the Author

Missouri Vaun grew up in rural southern Mississippi, where she spent lazy summers conjuring characters and imagining the worlds they might inhabit. It might be a little-known fact that Mississippi breeds eccentrics, and eccentrics make for good storytelling. Missouri spent twelve years finding her voice as a working journalist in places as disparate as Chicago and Jackson, Mississippi. Her stories are heartfelt, earthy, and speak of loyalty and our responsibility to others. She and her wife currently live in northern California. Missouri can be reached via email at Missouri.Vaun@gmail.com or via the Web at MissouriVaun.com.

Books Available From Bold Strokes Books

The Time Before Now by Missouri Vaun. Vivian flees a disastrous affair, embarking on an epic, transformative journey to escape her past, until destiny introduces her to Ida, who helps her rediscover trust, love, and hope. (978-1-62639-446-9)

Twisted Whispers by Sheri Lewis Wohl. Betrayal, lies, and secrets—whispers of a friend lost to darkness. Can a reluctant psychic set things right or will an evil soul destroy those she loves? (978-1-62639-439-1)

The Courage to Try by C.A. Popovich. Finding love is worth getting past the fear of trying. (978-1-62639-528-2)

Break Point by Yolanda Wallace. In a world readying for war, can love find a way? (978-1-62639-568-8)

Countdown by Julie Cannon. Can two strong-willed, powerful women overcome their differences to save the lives of seven others and begin a life they never imagined together? (978-1-62639-471-1)

Keep Hold by Michelle Grubb. Claire knew some things should be left alone and some rules should never be broken, but the most forbidden, well, they are the most tempting. (978-1-62639-502-2)

Deadly Medicine by Jaime Maddox. Dr. Ward Thrasher's life is in turmoil. Her partner Jess left her, and her job puts her in the path of a murderous physician who has Jess in his sights. (978-1-62639-424-7)

New Beginnings by KC Richardson. Can the connection and attraction between Jordan Roberts and Kirsten Murphy be enough for Jordan to trust Kirsten with her heart? (978-1-62639-450-6)

Officer Down by Erin Dutton. Can two women who've made careers out of being there for others in crisis find the strength to need each other? (978-1-62639-423-0)

Reasonable Doubt by Carsen Taite. Just when Sarah and Ellery think they've left dangerous careers behind, a new case sets them—and their hearts—on a collision course. (978-1-62639-442-1)

Tarnished Gold by Ann Aptaker. Cantor Gold must outsmart the Law, outrun New York's dockside gangsters, outplay a shady art dealer, his lover, and a beautiful curator, and stay out of a killer's gun sights. (978-1-62639-426-1)

The Renegade by Amy Dunne. Post-apocalyptic survivors Alex and Evelyn secretly find love while held captive by a deranged cult, but when their relationship is discovered, they must fight for their freedom—or die trying. (978-1-62639-427-8)

Thrall by Barbara Ann Wright. Four women in a warrior society must work together to lift an insidious curse while caught between their own desires, the will of their peoples, and an ancient evil. (978-1-62639-437-7)

White Horse in Winter by Franci McMahon. Love between two women collides with the inner poison of a closeted horse trainer in the green hills of Vermont. (978-1-62639-429-2)

Autumn Spring by Shelley Thrasher. Can Bree and Linda, two women in the autumn of their lives, put their hearts first and find the love they've never dared seize? (978-1-62639-365-3)

The Chameleon's Tale by Andrea Bramhall. Two old friends must work through a web of lies and deceit to find themselves again, but in the search they discover far more than they ever went looking for. (978-1-62639-363-9)

Side Effects by VK Powell. Detective Jordan Bishop and Dr. Neela Sahjani must decide if it's easier to trust someone with your heart or your life as they face threatening protestors, corrupt politicians, and their increasing attraction. (978-1-62639-364-6)

Warm November by Kathleen Knowles. What do you do if the one woman you want is the only one you can't have? (978-1-62639-366-0)

In Every Cloud by Tina Michele. When Bree finally leaves her shattered life behind, is she strong enough to salvage the remaining pieces of her heart and find the place where it truly fits? (978-1-62639-413-1)

Rise of the Gorgon by Tanai Walker. When independent Internet journalist Elle Pharell goes to Kuwait to investigate a veteran's mysterious suicide, she hires Cassandra Hunt, an interpreter with a covert agenda. (978-1-62639-367-7)

Crossed by Meredith Doench. Agent Luce Hansen returns home to catch a killer and risks everything to revisit the unsolved murder of her first girlfriend and confront the demons of her youth. (978-1-62639-361-5)

Making a Comeback by Julie Blair. Music and love take center stage when jazz pianist Liz Randall tries to make a comeback with the help of her reclusive, blind neighbor, Jac Winters. (978-1-62639-357-8)

Soul Unique by Gun Brooke. Self-proclaimed cynic Greer Landon falls for Hayden Rowe's paintings and the young woman shortly after, but will Hayden, who lives with Asperger syndrome, trust her and reciprocate her feelings? (978-1-62639-358-5)

The Price of Honor by Radclyffe. Honor and duty are not always black and white—and when self-styled patriots take up arms against the government, the price of honor may be a life. (978-1-62639-359-2)

Mounting Evidence by Karis Walsh. Lieutenant Abigail Hargrove and her mounted police unit need to solve a murder and protect wetland biologist Kira Lovell during the Washington State Fair. (978-1-62639-343-1)

Threads of the Heart by Jeannie Levig. Maggie and Addison Rae-McInnis share a love and a life, but are the threads that bind them together strong enough to withstand Addison's restlessness and the seductive Victoria Fontaine? (978-1-62639-410-0)

Sheltered Love by MJ Williamz. Boone Fairway and Grey Dawson—two women touched by abuse—overcome their pasts to find happiness in each other. (978-1-62639-362-2)

Death's Doorway by Crin Claxton. Helping the dead can be deadly: Tony may be listening to the dead, but she needs to learn to listen to the living. (978-1-62639-354-7)

Searching for Celia by Elizabeth Ridley. As American spy novelist Dayle Salvesen investigates the mysterious disappearance of her ex-lover, Celia, in London, she begins questioning how well she knew Celia—and how well she knows herself. (978-1-62639-356-1).

Hardwired by C.P. Rowlands. Award-winning teacher Clary Stone and Leefe Ellis, manager of the homeless shelter for small children, stand together in a part of Clary's hometown that she never knew existed. (978-1-62639-351-6)

The Muse by Meghan O'Brien. Erotica author Kate McMannis struggles with writer's block until a gorgeous muse entices her into a world of fantasy sex and inadvertent romance. (978-1-62639-223-6)

No Good Reason by Cari Hunter. A violent kidnapping in a Peak District village pushes Detective Sanne Jensen and lifelong friend Dr. Meg Fielding closer, just as it threatens to tear everything apart. (978-1-62639-352-3)

The 45th Parallel by Lisa Girolami. Burying her mother isn't the worst thing that can happen to Val Montague when she returns to the woodsy but peculiar town of Hemlock, Oregon. (978-1-62639-342-4)

Romance by the Book by Jo Victor. If Cam didn't keep disrupting her life, maybe Alex could uncover the secret of a century-old love story, and solve the greatest mystery of all—her own heart. (978-1-62639-353-0)

A Royal Romance by Jenny Frame. In a country where class still divides, can love topple the last social taboo and allow Queen Georgina and Beatrice Elliot, a working-class girl, their happy ever after? (978-1-62639-360-8)

Bouncing by Jaime Maddox. Basketball coach Alex Dalton has been bouncing from woman to woman because no one ever held her interest, until she meets her new assistant, Britain Dodge. (978-1-62639-344-8)

All Things Rise by Missouri Vaun. Cole rescues a striking pilot who crash-lands near her family's farm, setting in motion a chain of events that will forever alter the course of her life. (978-1-62639-346-2)